Retreat from Gettysburg

By
Kathleen Ernst

W︱M KIDS WHITE MANE KIDS

This White Mane Books publication
was printed by
Beidel Printing House, Inc.
63 West Burd Street
Shippensburg, PA 17257-0152 USA

In respect for the scholarship contained herein, the acid-free paper used in this book meets the guidelines for permanence and durability of the Committee on Production Guidelines for Book Longevity of the Council on Library Resources.

For a complete list of available publications
please write
White Mane Books
Division of White Mane Publishing Company, Inc.
P.O. Box 152
Shippensburg, PA 17257-0152 USA

Library of Congress Cataloging-in-Publication Data

Ernst, Kathleen, 1959-
    Retreat from Gettysburg / by Kathleen Ernst.
        p. cm.
    Includes bibliographical references.
    Summary: In 1863, during the tense week after the Battle of Gettysburg, a Maryland boy faces difficult choices as he is forced to care for a wounded Confederate officer while trying to decide if he himself should leave his family to fight for the Union.
    ISBN 1-57249-187-6 (alk. paper)
    1. Gettysburg (Pa.), Battle of, 1863--Juvenile fiction. [1. Gettysburg (Pa.), Battle of, 1863---Fiction. 2. United States--History--Civil War, 1861-1865--Campaigns--Fiction.] I. Title.

PZ7.E7315 Re 2000
[Fic]--dc21

                                                                    99-057810

For Matthew, Rachel, Hunter, and Julia

CONTENTS

List of Illustrations vi
Acknowledgments vii
Chapter 1   July 4–5, 1863 1
Chapter 2   July 5, 1863 11
Chapter 3   July 6, 1863 17
Chapter 4   July 6, 1863 23
Chapter 5   July 6, 1863 33
Chapter 6   July 6, 1863 39
Chapter 7   July 7, 1863 43
Chapter 8   July 8, 1863 51
Chapter 9   July 8–9, 1863 60
Chapter 10   July 10–11, 1863 65
Chapter 11   July 12, 1863 71
Chapter 12   July 12, 1863 81
Chapter 13   July 13, 1863 86
Chapter 14   July 13, 1863 97
Chapter 15   July 13, 1863 102
Chapter 16   July 13–14, 1863 108
Chapter 17   July 14–15, 1863 118
Chapter 18   July 15–19, 1863 127
Afterward 133
Author's Note 135
Additional Resources 140

*I*LLUSTRATIONS

Route of the Confederate ambulance train x

Two views of Williamsport's warehouse basin 3

The ferry and ford at Williamsport, Maryland 15

Confederate army crossing the Potomac River 45

Confederate Brigadier General John Imboden 94

Confederate troops retreating from Gettysburg,
  Pennsylvania 95

6th Michigan Cavalry at Falling Waters, Virginia 113

Confederate Brigadier General Johnston Pettigrew 114

Yankee troops crossing the C & O Canal and
  the Potomac River 132

ACKNOWLEDGMENTS

I am indebted to a number of people who helped bring this book to life. Sue Ann Sullivan shared a number of resources with me, and offered her services as guide to Williamsport, Maryland. Eric Wittenberg generously shared a portion of his then-unpublished manuscript, featuring the letters of James H. Kidd of the 6th Michigan, which provided insight into the cavalry charge at Falling Waters, Virginia. Local historian John Frye was kind enough to review the manuscript while in draft stage, and caught several errors I might have overlooked.

D. Scott Hartwig, historian at Gettysburg National Military Park, also took time from his busy personal schedule to review the manuscript. John Heiser, librarian at Gettysburg National Military Park, helped locate several military accounts that shed light on the final days of the Gettysburg campaign. Douglas Stover, chief of Cultural Resources Management for the C & O Canal National Historic Park, helped identify historic photographs and shared a wonderfully detailed history of Williamsport from the park service files.

I'm fortunate to have the support of my talented friends in the WCR: Eileen Daily, Amy Laundrie, Julia Pferdehirt, and Gayle Rosengren. And I appreciate Renee Raduechel's careful eye.

As always, I feel very grateful to my family for their constant encouragement. Special thanks go to my husband, Scott Meeker, who has spent several years lugging boxes of books, proofreading manuscripts, killing time at book signings, planning vacation time around my research needs, and living with a variety of other inconveniences stemming from my writing. I couldn't ask for a better partner.

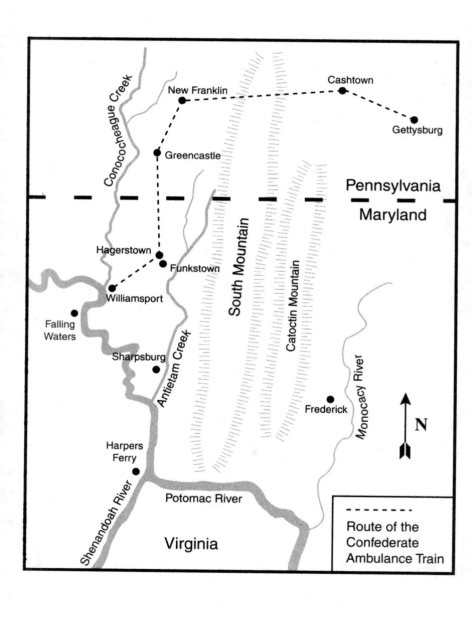

CHAPTER ONE

JULY 4–5, 1863

The rain came so fast, so hard, I thought it was a God-sent curse. I'd never seen such a fierce rain, and I'd lived in Williamsport for all my fourteen years.

Lots of country folks had come to town for news of the big battle fought during the first three days of July at some little Pennsylvania town called Gettysburg, just north of the Maryland line. They shivered in the downpour, waiting for the lists of dead and wounded to get posted. I had no name left to look for in the lists. But I had stood in those waiting crowds too, too many times. I knew they'd stand so for days, if need be, rain or no.

Williamsport squats on the banks of the C & O Canal and the Potomac River beyond. Confederate Virginia was right across the Potomac from us in Maryland. The new Confederacy was fighting the American Union. We called the Confederates "cursed Rebels," and the Potomac was all that came between us and them. It was a mighty important river.

I knew that river as well as any of the other boys thereabouts. But I didn't know the Potomac after two days and nights of fierce rain. It rose and raged like an angry beast. It

1

swallowed the cable the ferryman used to haul his flatboat back and forth near the ford. It swept away parts of the canal itself, and Mansfield's canalboat and livelihood along with it, and one more family packed up to leave Williamsport. It rammed through Robert Kincaid's shack and muleshed. Robert had used his mules to tow boats down the canal before some soldiers broke in and stole them all, leaving him nothing but an empty stall. Once the Potomac came through, he didn't even have that.

The rain did dull the smell of the butchered cow carcasses left ringing our village by the cursed Rebels when they'd moved through two weeks earlier, and with it the incessant buzzing of flies. But when the waters grew high enough some of those carcasses began to float, staring eyeballs and maggots and all. Most of them went down the river, and we wished them well on the Confederates. But one ended up on the Ainsmingers' front porch, and one somehow got wedged over the Huxleys' well so the water wasn't fit to drink. The Huxleys were Rebel sympathizers, so I didn't care.

On the Fourth of July I climbed Cemetery Hill, which hunches between the town and the canal, and watched the river rise. "Looks like I won't be going fishing for a while," I told my father's grave. "River's in flood." I brushed some sticks and leaves from his grave and the two graves beyond it, and straightened the cross I'd pounded into the ground to mark the empty spot just beyond those. Those graves were well-tended because I visited often.

"I'm still trying to sort out what to do, Pa," I added, picking up the conversation where last we'd left off. "I know you likely want me to enlist. But Ma's the thing. Sometimes her anger's a fiery thing. I'm glad of it. Anger means there's still a...a spark inside. But sometimes I'm feared she's going to lose—"

"Hey, Chigger."

In the rain, I hadn't heard Robert Kincaid hauling himself up the slippery slope to join me. Robert had looked

Two postwar views of the Potomac River, C & O Canal, and the warehouse basin where canalboats stopped to unload their cargo. Top: This 1872 sketch shows a warehouse in detail, and the aqueduct which carried the canal over Conococheague Creek. Railroad service didn't reach Williamsport, Maryland, until after the Civil War. Bottom: Taken from Cemetery Hill, this 1900 photograph gives a better perspective of the Potomac River (at left), the C & O Canal, and the canal towpath. Just visible at the right is the warehouse basin.

C & O Canal National Historic Park

mournful ever since his mules got stolen—they were all he had, and he'd set quite a store by them. But I couldn't help noticing that half-drowned, he looked more miserable than ever.

"I heard about your shed washing away," I said, "and I'm real sorry for it. You got a place to sleep? You can sleep in our stable, if you like. The roof's starting to cave in at the east end. But the west corner's still dry."

It may not seem like much of an offer. But we had rain trouble at our little place too, half a mile down river of town. The rain beat through the loose shingles on our cow shed. Since we didn't have any cows left, I didn't see much reason to mind. But in our cabin the floorboards had turned green with mold, rotting from the ground up. That did matter. I was the only man left on the place, and responsible for such. But I didn't have a notion what to do about it, so it went untended. A stable corner was the best I had to offer.

Robert brightened. "That's real kind of you, Chig. Real kind."

"Are you finding any work?" I asked. I knew he'd been struggling to hold body and soul together since his mules got stolen.

He shrugged. "Some. Old farmer Ballweg said he'd hire me on to cut wheat, if the rain ever lets up." Gloom slipped back over his face. Robert didn't much cotton to farmwork. Me, I would have taken the job in a blink.

Robert turned and squinted into the driving rain. "What can you see?" he asked. Robert was blind in one eye.

"Potomac's five foot deep at Embry's Warehouse," I told him. "Ruined whatever they didn't get hauled to higher ground." The warehouse was in the loading basin, where the canalboats' cargo was stored until it was hauled off. There were only a couple of warehouses left, since some Yankees—that's what the Union soldiers were called—had burned most of them the year before to keep them from Rebel hands.

"I got hired yesterday to help haul at Embry's." Robert shook his head. "We got a lot moved, but three boatloads of coal and plaster got ruined."

I wished I had known the warehouse men were hiring. I was a few years younger than Robert, and the farmers looking for hired hands thought me too small, but I might have earned a few pennies at the warehouse. I needed the money. If I didn't join the army, chances were good I'd have to leave home anyway to look for work. And where would that leave Ma?

By the next day the Conococheague Creek, which meets the Potomac on the north edge of town, was pouring over its banks. Up near Middlekauff's Mill, where Agnes and my new nephew-baby Willis lived, the overflow swept through and washed the last few young turnips right out of the garden. I happened by, slogging ankle deep, right as the vegetables went bobbing down Clear Spring Road. Widow Ainsminger was passing too, and dove after those turnips quicker than a hawk on mice.

Just then Agnes's father, Dr. Conrad, staggered out of the house with Mrs. Conrad in his arms to keep her from the muck. He headed toward his buggy. "Morning, Chigger," he puffed, while the rain spattered off his old top hat. "You on an errand, or just walking?"

"Just walking." I wiped a stream of cold rain from my eyes.

"How's your mama holding up?"

"Tolerable." That was a stretch. But what ailed Ma, Dr. Conrad couldn't cure.

Dr. Conrad stumbled, then regained his footing. "I'm taking Mrs. Conrad to higher ground."

"Agnes going too?" I hardly knew Agnes, though she'd married my brother Liam early last October and borne his son nine months later. Still, if she and baby Willis were leaving town, it seemed fitting for me to know.

"She said she's staying put," Dr. Conrad puffed, blinking as raindrops streaked down his spectacles. "Weather's not fit for a newborn."

I tried to figure out how I could ease his way, for Mrs. Conrad was a round heap of skirts and pettiskirts and looked to be a bit much for her husband. Mrs. Conrad set me straight. "Don't just stand there, boy," she said. "It would be a help if you fetched my bag." I saw a valise waiting on the step, just above the waterline, and humped it over to the buggy. Mrs. Conrad's bonnet somehow came loose as her husband shoved her up on the seat, and I fished it from the water for her too. She settled the muddy thing back on her head and in that soggy style, the Conrads set out. The mule pulling their wagon was too miserable for the army to steal, and I hoped he lasted 'til they found that higher ground she wanted.

After watching them go I squinted for a minute at the pretty frame house where the Conrads lived, then waded to the front step and knocked on the door. After a bit Agnes opened it. I got just a peek at Willis, wrapped in a blanket and held over one shoulder.

"Chigger O'Malley!" Agnes sounded surprised. She was a plain, quiet girl, but never-fail polite. "What are you doing here? Do you want to come in?"

"No." I saw no call to drip all over her nice carpet. "I chanced to see your folks head out. Thought I'd see if you needed anything. You and the baby."

"We'll be all right. I don't suspect the water'll rise over the step. If it does, we'll just go upstairs."

I nodded. There wasn't anything I could have done for them anyway, but I *was* Willis's uncle. I felt an obligation to ask, with her father leaving and all. It was a gesture, as Ma would say. All I had to offer.

Agnes closed the door, and I waded back to the street and started walking again. The Conrads weren't the only folks skedaddling. I saw what happened thereabouts because when I wasn't fishing I walked the village streets and country lanes. Every day. Even in the flooding rain. A body does strange things, I guess, when he has too much time and too much quiet at home.

Still, though I sometimes wished to, I couldn't stay out all day. Ma had gone quiet after I'd seen her home from Sunday mass that morning. I hadn't been able to find the words to pull her out of it, so I'd left. After seeing Agnes, I spent another half-hour walking and thinking and scraping up the resolve to go back home and try again.

After two days of rain the road past our cabin was knee-deep in sucking, slimy mud. I found Ma there on her hands and knees, crouched like a dog waiting to be kicked again, while the rain slashed down. "Ma!" I cried, dropping down beside her. "What happened?"

She blinked like I was a stranger. "I was looking for that Leghorn," she said finally. "The mud...I lost my footing."

I shook my head, pulling her up. That skinny Leghorn was the last chicken we had left after two years of war. "How long you been out here, Ma?"

She didn't seem to know. It took me a right smart while to tug her down our lane and into the house.

If Father Ryan had been there I'd have asked why God sent the infernal rain to us, after everything else we'd been through. But Father Ryan wasn't there, so I boiled up some tea for Ma, and wrapped an old quilt around her shoulders, and found a tin bowl to set under the newest leak in the corner, just over my bed.

You can see why we thought that rain was a curse.

But then the rain stopped, and the *real* curse arrived.

It came late that afternoon in the form of the Rebel army, moving fast and grim. We'd heard they'd just been beat, beat bad, at this Gettysburg place. That was the first good news I could remember. Those Rebels wanted nothing more than to cross the Potomac River back into Virginia, their own home soil of the Confederacy. They'd been bloodied and battered, it was plain to see. The Yankees, we heard, were close on their heels. If the Yankees moved quick enough, they could gobble those Rebels up and end the war once and for all.

There was nothing I wanted more. I wanted the war to be over. And I wanted every cursed Rebel to pay for what they'd done to my family. And so I prayed long and hard for the rain to keep coming, and for the river to stay high.

When I wandered back to town for a look-see, the first Rebels I saw were cavalry, lean and ragged and hungry-looking as wolves, riding mud-caked horses that looked hard used. They headed straight toward the ford, a natural shallow place where a man could usually splash across no more than hip-deep. Now they pulled up, staring at the raging river in flood. It was ten feet above flood stage, ready to swallow any man foolish enough to try to cross, even the strongest rower in the sturdiest boat.

"You! Boy!"

I jumped, realizing one of them was calling me. Williamsport being right on the river, at a natural crossing spot, I'd been watching soldiers come and go through two years of war. I generally knew how to stay out of sight and out of trouble. "What?"

"Is this the ford?" The rider peered at me from beneath the dripping brim of a shapeless hat the color of mud.

I shrugged. "It was two days ago."

"What about the pontoon bridge?"

"It was a few miles downstream. Across from Falling Waters. But some Yankee riders broke it up." I kept my voice even, hands in pockets, so when the Rebel cursed, it wasn't aimed at me. Inside, I wanted to whoop. The Rebels were trapped. They had built the pontoon bridge when they'd plunged across the Potomac on their way to Gettysburg, and I knew they were figuring on using it to get back to safety. I guess they hadn't heard that some Yankees stationed in nearby Frederick City had come and chopped the string of boats and planking to pieces while the Rebels were tramping through Pennsylvania.

Those Rebel riders were escorting a wagon train that stretched, I heard later, for seventeen miles. It took a long time to manhandle those wagons into town. Their wheels churned through the mud and got stuck and made deep ruts sure to trip whoever came through next. And except for a few loads of flour and coffee and sugar, those wagons were stuffed with wounded Rebels. Thousands of them, shot up at Gettysburg. I got close enough to hear the groans.

When officers began pounding on folks' doors, shouting that they had better start cooking up everything they had for the wounded, I figured it was time to quit wandering and head home again. I found Ma standing in the doorway arguing with one of the rangy, thieving, murdering Rebels.

"I won't cook for any cursed Rebs," she was saying.

"You'll cook for us or we'll turn you out and take over your kitchen ourselves."

"You've been through here before. Taken everything we had and more. Dug up our garden. Stolen our chickens and cow. We're starving already."

"Cook up what you got."

"We've got nothing!"

The man's eyes narrowed. "I'll be back through in an hour. See you have something to give."

"I've already given it all," Ma moaned, but the Rebel was already wading back across the yard. He struggled and almost lost his balance as the mud sucked at his boots, and I hoped he would fall facedown and drown in the slimy ooze. But he didn't, and I had Ma to tend to. "You've still got me, Ma," I reminded her, though I knew that was sorry comfort for what she'd been through.

"Yes," she whispered, clenching my hand so hard it hurt. "You're all I've got left, Chigger. Promise me you won't go."

"I won't go," I repeated, steering her toward the pantry shelf. Usually that promise knocked in my head like a hammer, for in my heart of hearts, I didn't know what to do. Join the Yankee army's Irish Brigade and avenge the dead O'Malleys? Stay and try to keep Ma from giving in altogether?

But for the moment, I shoved that question aside. I was full up wondering if cooking for the Rebels truly would starve us proper this time. My belly button was knocking against my backbone as it was. With the river so high, I couldn't fish. We'd seen hard times. The arrival of these Rebels promised worse.

Then I lined my thoughts up proper. Even going hungry didn't seem too important, after what the Rebels had already done. And the rain, which had flooded the Potomac and trapped the Rebels like treed coons while the Yankees hunted them down, I came to see as a God-sent blessing. General Lee's whole Rebel army was fixed to pour into Williamsport behind that train of wounded. The Yankees weren't far behind, folks said. It was only a matter of time until everything was over.

The end of the war! Right there at Williamsport. It was a heady promise. Still, some people were nervy about it. I'd heard them muttering. A big fight had come in nearby Sharpsburg the year before, and Sharpsburg folks'd had the devil to pay for months afterwards: tons of manure from all the armies' horses, thousands of dead to bury, thousands of wounded to tend, farmfolks' root cellars and stables emptied out and winter coming on. "We can't survive that," I had heard Father Ryan say, when word came to Williamsport that the Rebels were on their way, retreating from Gettysburg.

I didn't care. We had little enough left anyway, with all the soldiers passing through. Hungry, hard-marching men, the lot of 'em.

Let the battle come, I thought. That would be enough to avenge the O'Malleys. It might even be enough to keep Ma from slipping away to some hidden place in her mind, where I couldn't follow. Let it come and may every murdering Rebel get killed right there in Williamsport. I wanted to watch.

There was nothing to do but wait.

CHAPTER TWO

JULY 5, 1863

Ma was right: we didn't have much left. My pa had made a proper living, working sometimes as a canal laborer and sometimes in the cement mill just upstream. We'd never been rich, not with four hungry boys in the family. But we'd always gotten by. I hadn't known what a true worry was when Pa was still alive, and Egan, and Patrick, and Liam. Then we had pork and gravy at least once a week, and stewed chicken and dumplings every Sunday after mass. We had fresh greens from the garden in summer and crocks of gooseberry preserves and dried apples to see us through the cold months.

And we had *noise*. Sometimes arguing, more often laughter, but always someone trying to be heard. That day, there was nothing to hear as Mama cooked up a little cornbread. When the Rebel came back, I shoved it at him and slammed the door. "He's gone, Ma," I said, when I turned back to the little room.

Ma sank into the rocking chair in the corner. "Do you have your boat well hid, Chig? They'll be wanting boats."

"Yes." Truth was, I wasn't sure. I'd spent the better part of an afternoon dragging my rowboat across the canal and deep into the woods above the spot where I usually put in. But I'd been thinking to keep it from the floodwater's reach, not the Rebels'. Was it hid well enough? Doubt poked my insides.

I didn't want to lose that rowboat. It had been my pa's. He'd taught me to know this stretch of the Potomac well: the sandbars, the rocks, the current, the good fishing holes. I pulled in catfish, crappies, pickerel, sometimes bass. Eels too, during spring spawning season. The fish had been standing between us and pure hunger. The thought of losing the boat to the cursed Rebels didn't set well.

But I didn't say so. It was a habit I'd gotten into, telling my mother what she wanted to hear. At first light I'd go check the boat, make sure it was safe hid. "They won't find it, Ma," I said firmly. "Only Rebels here so far are the wounded and an escort of cavalry and some infantry. Rest of 'em are close behind, though, from what they're saying in town. I'm thinking they'll be trapped until the Yankees get here to kill them all. End the war."

She didn't bother to answer.

I waited a moment. "Can I get you something?"

She didn't answer that either.

I sighed and went into the lean-to that served as kitchen. The fire in the cookstove had about died and I tried to blow it back to life, but all our kindling was damp. I washed up the dirty dishes with cold water. They still seemed a bit slimy when I was done, but I put them on the shelf anyway.

Then I peeked through the door at Ma. She was staring at the wall. Was that better than staring at the tintypes of my father and brothers, like she sometimes did? They had all left some distant training camp in their new Yankee uniforms to find a photographic studio, where their images had been captured on the dull bits of tin. They'd sent them back with letters that said things like, "Don't I look handsome in my uniform?" And, "There's rumors of a coming battle. I thought you might like my likeness."

And one by one had come the other letters, written by strangers, which all began something like this: "I am sorry to write you with grievous news..." And soon new black crepe was draping one of the tintypes, because another O'Malley was dead.

Pa and Egan had left together in 1861. They joined a unit called the Irish Brigade, and died within a week of each other, after a battle the newspapers called Bull Run.

After we buried them Patrick had trudged away to war, vowing vengeance. He joined my pa's old friends in the Irish Brigade, and was killed within a year himself. He was shot just a few miles away at Sharpsburg, during the battle of Antietam Creek, in September 1862.

And Liam, he enlisted quietly soon after that. He up and married his Agnes before he left, which was a surprise, her being Methodist and all. He was dead by spring. He was seventeen.

The tintypes were all on the mantelpiece now, framed in little brass holders with flags and drums hammered in relief on them, draped in the black crepe. They commanded the room. From where I stood watching Ma, the only other thing I could see was the fiddle hanging on the wall. I had a sudden urge to cut a strip of that black fabric and fling it over the fiddle.

You see, Ma played the fiddle. Before the war, she used to play all the time: sweet lullabies at bedtime, light airs on sunny spring afternoons, cheerful jigs and reels she recalled from Ireland on cold winter nights when the wind howled around the eaves.

Sometimes friends had crammed inside our tiny house and teased her to play. She always started with some quiet tunes, and I'd sit in the corner and watch the smile tease her lips while the others got restless. Finally someone would yell, "Maureen, *saw* that thing!" and then she'd let go. And soon folks were singing and stomping and howling, and someone would start dancing, and if the weather was fair the dancing spilled out into the yard. Pa wasn't much of a singer but he could dance, and the boys always danced with the girls, swinging them until they squealed and we all saw a bit more ankle and petticoat than was considered proper. I stayed in my corner and watched it all, content. *Safe.* My ma's a wee scrap of a woman but she'd tap her foot lively while she played, and sometimes jump up and down like the music was spilling out from the inside. Mama fiddled like she thought her music was all that stood between us and the end of the world.

When Pa and Egan walked out of our house for the last time, she played an old Irish song to let them know her stout heart was with them:

> *For fighting, for drinking, for ladies and all,*
> *No time like our times e'er was made, O,*
> *By the rollicking boys, for war, for ladies and noise,*
> *The boys of the Irish Brigade, O!*

She stopped playing lively when they were out of sight. Night after night she let her fingers slide across the strings only in soft songs of loneliness. Then the first letter came, and the first strip of black mourning crepe got cut. The second letter. The second strip of crepe. And soon after two sealed-tight coffins arrived by canalboat. She played a mournful dirge at the wake:

> *And all you boys, do take my advice*
> *To America I'll have you not be comin'*
> *For there's nothing here but war*
> *Where the murderin' cannons roar*
> *And I wish I was back home in dear old Ireland.*

And when Pa and Egan were buried in those coffins on top of Cemetery Hill, she stopped playing altogether.

Some time after that, back in 1861, a band of thieving Rebels had slipped across the river and come pounding down our road looking for whatever they could plunder. Patrick and Liam were at work, and Ma grabbed my shoulder. "Run inside, grab what you can, and hide," she'd hissed.

During the Civil War, troops often used the ferry and ford at Williamsport. This early-war sketch shows a military band playing on the Virginia shore while Union troops cross the river.

Sketch by Edwin Forbes, *Harper's Weekly*; courtesy Frank & Marie-Therese Wood Print Collection, Alexandria, Virginia.

She ran on to the stable, hoping to save the cow, while I darted inside. I wasn't so used to soldiers then, and I recall looking around wildly, heart pounding and scared from top to bottom. Finally I grabbed the fiddle, ran out, and hid in the woods.

When the soldiers had come and gone, and I came back, she scolded me: "We can't eat a fiddle!"

I didn't know how to tell her that I'd rather live with the hunger in my belly than the screaming silence in our house.

The next time soldiers came, Patrick was gone to war too, and Liam was away courting Agnes. Some Yankee stragglers, no-goods shaming their blue uniforms, caught us by surprise. One marched right inside, where Ma and I were sitting down to dinner. He filled a sack with all the food he could grab. Some rutabagas and potatoes and cheese, I recall. Then his eyes lit on the fiddle.

He was reaching for it when Ma snatched up the bow and threatened him with it like it was a whip. "Don't dare touch it."

He laughed. "I've been missing my own fiddle, woman. I'll just be—"

Ma brought the bow down across the back of his hand like a bitter schoolmarm. *Whack!* I sucked my breath into the pit of my stomach, wondering if Ma was about to be shot stone dead in front of me. For a long moment that soldier stared from the welt on his hand to Ma and back again, his jaw sagging open. Finally, he shoved that hand in his pocket, picked up the foodsack with the other hand, and walked out the door.

So I knew Ma still had a bit of her heart locked inside that fiddle. Sometimes I begged her to play. Most often she just shook her head. Then I asked once too often. *"How can I?"* she blazed, turning on me, her eyes like glowing coals. *"Don't ever ask me again!"* Her voice was harsh and raspy, like the devil himself was pulling a bow across fiddle strings.

So the fiddle hung on the wall.

And when I counted up the sins of the Rebels, after killing my pa and my brother Egan and my brother Patrick and my brother Liam, I added eternal silence to the list. And I hated them no less for that than the other murders I laid at their door.

CHAPTER THREE

JULY 6, 1863

The night after the wagon train of wounded Rebels arrived back from Gettysburg I dreamed of Ma and her fiddle. She was playing a lively jig. Egan and Patrick and Liam were all clapping their hands and hooting, grinning, very alive. Pa shouted, "*Saw* that thing, Maureen!" and began stomping one booted foot on the floor in time with the beat. But too soon the fiddle music faded, and all I could hear was Pa stomping...

I jerked awake and realized the stomping was, after all, someone pounding on our front door. The first gray light of a new morn was creeping across the moldy floorboards. Ma crouched beside the pallet of blankets on the floor where I slept, and shook my shoulder. "Chig, get up. Trouble." She was dressed, but her hair hung down her back in a loose braid.

"What is it?" I jumped to my feet, quick pulled on my trousers, and fastened the suspenders—all that held them up, these days.

"I don't know. See to the door."

My heart was pounding like the fist of whoever was beyond the door. In the seconds it took to open the door I wondered if my brothers would have been scared, if they were still alive. I didn't think so. They'd all screwed up the courage to enlist in the Union army, after all...especially Patrick and Liam, who knew when they left that wars were not about fun and glory after all.

I found three Rebels on the front step. The man in front had gray hair, and dark pouches under bloodshot eyes, and looked unsteady on his feet. He was either a drinker or plum exhausted. "I'm Surgeon Hatfield," he said. "I've a wagon full of wounded men to find shelter for. How many can you take in?"

Take in? A surge of hatred inside burned away my fear. "None!"

"This is a Union house," Ma added behind me, in a tone that would have sent any O'Malley male running for cover.

But the doctor didn't care a whit for an Irish woman's ire. "Good Lord, madam," he snapped, "I've got men dying here!" He shoved me aside and motioned behind him. "Sergeant Krick! Bring Captain Tallard in."

One of the soldiers behind him was supporting the other, Tallard. The hurt man's head wobbled toward his chest. He wasn't wearing a jacket, just a dirty old homespun blouse with a bloodstain off to one side. Then I noticed he only had one arm. His left arm ended just above the elbow.

Surgeon Hatfield pointed at my mother's bed in the corner. "Put him there."

My hands balled into fists. "You can't—"

"Hush your trap, boy, 'fore I hush it for you," Sergeant Krick grunted. He was a big man, with black hair and a fierce bruise on one cheek and a toothbrush dangling from a buttonhole. It seemed the oddest thing, seeing that toothbrush hanging against the muddy rags of his uniform.

He eased Tallard down on the blankets. "There you be, George," he said, his voice suddenly softer. He took a moment to push a pillow beneath the bandaged stump where Tallard's arm had been. "You'll be able to dry out here. Get some rest. I'll come see to you when I can."

The surgeon was stalking around the room, looking in all the corners. A moment later he was in the kitchen, opening drawers, banging cupboard doors.

"You're going to rob us even as you leave one of your own in this house?" Ma demanded. She had backed against a wall, arms hugged across her chest.

"No," he said shortly. And to Krick, "Fetch them in a sack of flour, and some coffee and sugar. There isn't food to feed a mouse."

Krick nodded. "Is it just the captain, then? Or should I get another man from the wagon?"

"There's no room in here for more." Surgeon Hatfield took off his grimy hat and ran a hand through his hair. It splayed out in odd points, stiff and dirty, until he slapped his hat back on. "Is there a decent stable outside? Corncrib? Pig pen, even? We've got to get those men out of the rain!"

Krick shook his head. "Roof's falling in on the stable, and there's nothing else."

Krick had already checked the stable? I wondered if he'd crashed in on Robert, asleep in the straw. If so, Robert was no doubt a mile away by now. Robert didn't cotton to soldiers.

"We've no man left to tend the place." Ma's voice was cold as January ice. "You Rebels have killed them all."

I drew a deep breath, working at one of the punky places in the floor with a toe. *I* was the man of the place...wasn't I? That's what Ma said all the time, when she begged me not to go off like the others.

"I'm sorry for your troubles," Hatfield said, sounding weary. "But I can't help you." He pointed at the crucifix on the wall. "This is a Christian house? Well, do your Christian duty. Tend this man, best you can. I'll stop back when I can to check on him. Keep the stump elevated. Let him have water or a bit of bread if he'll take it. Wine would be better, if you have some hidden away."

After they left, Krick came back with a sack of provisions and dumped them on the floor. "You folks can share, but make sure our man gets what he needs." He fixed me with a look that silenced my protest. "Boy, I'll be back this way. If I find you didn't tend that man well, I'll blow your head off."

Ma's hand landed on my shoulder as Krick left, her fingers biting like talons. "Don't make trouble, Chig. You're all I have left."

I stood for a moment, watching several scarecrow Rebels working to get the ambulance wagon out front moving again. It had sunk hub-deep in the ooze, and two men were wrestling planks under the wheels to give purchase while another whipped the skinny mules hitched in front, cursing like the devil. I wished the earth would swallow the wagon whole, with the wounded inside, all sucked down to the fiery pits of Hell where they belonged.

Then I slammed the door. And the three of us were alone: me, Ma, and the Rebel.

Ma stared for a moment, then stalked into the kitchen. She looked like an angry crow in the rusty black dress of mourning she'd been wearing day-in day-out for two years. I followed her and watched as she leaned against the wall, as far from the door into the main room as she could be. Then, all the anger seemed to sag from her body, and her fight with it. I bolted forward as her knees buckled and she slid slowly down in a heap. "Ma! Are you faint?"

"No. I just…I can't bear the sight of that murdering Rebel. In my own house! In my own bed! All my boys were born in that bed, Chig. My boys—" Her voice broke and she buried her face in her hands.

I didn't know what to do. I touched her shoulder, but she didn't move. I'm all the protection she has left, I thought, and wished I knew what in the blazes I could do for her. Would the arrival of this Rebel crush the last spark of light out of her? Would she finally just give up, slip away from me for good?

I padded back into the main room and sidled toward the bed, staring at Tallard. I'd seen Rebels, many times. The sight always brought out a civil war within me of hatred and fear. But this one was wounded, weak as a newborn pup by the looks of it. He couldn't hurt me.

But I could hurt him.

The thought hooked on my brain like a catfish on bait. I took another step toward the bed.

The man lying there was barefoot, wearing only his ragged trousers and the bloody shirt, caked high with mud. He was not young like my brothers, or nearing forty like Pa had been, but somewhere in between. He had dark hair and sunken cheeks and a fuzz of beard on his chin. His eyes had been closed, but they drifted open while I stared. "Sorry...to be of trouble," he mumbled.

As if an apology could undo the damage he and his kind had done!

I heard again the words that man Krick had hissed at me: *If I find you didn't tend that man well, I'll blow your head off...* I believed him. Yet, would he know? Could he know, with thousands of wounded Rebels in Williamsport and not enough beds, homes, stables to give shelter to even half that number? Maybe I could get away with it. Maybe I *should* do it, to avenge the dead O'Malley men staring down from the mantle.

My words formed defiant, but came out a whisper. "I could kill you right here."

The Rebel looked at me for a long moment, then closed his eyes. "Yes," he sighed. "You could."

I heard the heavy rasp of his breathing. A tiny, muffled sob from the kitchen. The plop of water dripping through one of the leak holes. I sucked in a big breath, wondering how to do it. A pistol shot would be quick and easy—but some passing Rebels might hear the shot, and besides, I didn't have a pistol. A pillow pressed against the face? That did not seem quick and easy, and the Rebel might struggle, fight, scream even...

Then I thought of something else. Keep the stump of his arm elevated, the doctor had said. What would happen if it wasn't? Would all Tallard's Rebel blood run from the end, until he died?

I reached out and curled my fingers around the stiff seam in the ticking-cloth of that pillow holding up what was left of Tallard's arm. Pinched it tight...

And jerked it away.

"Aahhh!" As Tallard's arm flopped down on the bed his eyes flew open, black with pain and surprise, drilling into me.

I dropped the pillow beside the bed and fled from the cabin.

CHAPTER FOUR

JULY 6, 1863

I slipped before I was halfway across the front yard and fell facedown into the muck. Scrambling to my feet, spitting mud, I kept going. I almost expected a hail of bullets from some hidden Rebel sharpshooter who somehow knew what I had done. My bare toes scrabbled for purchase, and once or twice I had to put a hand down to keep from falling again. But I kept running, down our lane and onto the main road.

When I finally stopped my chest was heaving. I leaned against a big walnut tree and braced my hands on my knees. I hadn't had breakfast, but my stomach suddenly tried mightily to heave up anything left from yesterday's meal.

So, I thought, when the world stopped quivering and I could finally draw an even breath. So, I guess I have killed a man. I pictured that Reb Tallard's blood pouring out, soaking into the sheets of the bed where Ma had borne all us boys. Was he dead yet? I didn't know how long such things took.

Did killing him make me a soldier? I thought of Pa and my brothers and wondered how many Rebels they'd killed. They hadn't written of such in the letters that had found their way home. I wished they were there to tell me what they'd

23

thought about the killing. How they'd felt about it. So far, killing Tallard just made me feel like I'd eaten too many sugared figs, like I had one Christmas before the war. Well, at least I'd avenged one O'Malley death. Maybe I wouldn't feel truly free of their beyond-the-grave expectations, truly like a soldier, until I'd avenged the other three dead O'Malleys too.

I'd think about that later. Right now, I had to think about what that Sergeant Krick would do when he came back and found Tallard dead. *I'll blow your head off...*

But he couldn't blame me, could he? How could he know? I'd say Tallard must have knocked the pillow to the floor himself. He'd been thrashing about in pain. And he'd bled to death before Ma or I knew what was what.

It was a fair story, sure enough. So why was I still feeling as shivery as if I'd fallen through Potomac ice on a February day?

Crimus! My shivers made me angry. Was I a wee boy, or the only O'Malley man left? I stuffed my hands in my pockets and began walking again, the question clanging in my head like bells at mass time, wishing like anything that I knew the answer.

I wasn't ready to head back to the cabin, and besides, I wanted to check on my rowboat. So I tramped on, away from town. When I passed a squad of Rebs heading north from Falling Waters, I stepped off the road and eyed the mud at my toes. Would one of them look at me and know what I'd done? See it in me? My stomach started churning again but they shuffled on by without a glance.

A mile from home, I cut to the Potomac. The boat was usually moored to a leaning sycamore in a quiet bend below town. When the rains came and the river started to rise I had dragged it over the canal and up the slope to a spot surely beyond high water, and snubbed it good in a sumac thicket. Now, relief flooded me when I pushed through the underbrush and saw it resting keel up where I'd left it.

Like I said, it had been my father's boat. One by one he'd taught his sons to know the river, and to fish. I never slipped the oars into the locks without hearing Pa's laugh, and feeling a lump rise in my throat. But I never felt closer to Pa's memory than when I was in that boat too, so I didn't aim to let the Rebels have it. I spent some time kicking up the grass plowed flat when I'd heaved the boat up the bank, and dragged some downed brush over the path too for good measure.

I felt good about that, but my mind kept swooping like a nuthatch back to the cabin. Was Tallard dead yet? Had Ma come from the kitchen? What would she do when she found the man bled to death in her own bed? Would she be happy? Satisfied? Or…

I started feeling shivery again, and without stewing about it any longer, decided to go to town and look for help. I didn't want to go back and face…face *whatever*, alone.

Williamsport was a little town, but already a century old. Indians, and later white settlers, had canoed down the Conococheague Creek and used the handy ford across the Potomac nearby. Soon a cable strung high across the river allowed men to ferry boats across. The C & O Canal, built in the 1830s and '40s, brought more traffic to Williamsport. Farmers' grain was floated down the Conococheague, and coal and crushed limestone down the canal from Cumberland and Hancock, to the waiting warehouses. Cushwa's tannery was big business. So was the cement mill upstream. Before the war Williamsport had been full of life and noise, and not all of it came from industry. A racetrack had been smoothed out on the level ground between the canal and the Potomac, just downstream from the Conococheague. So many people kept cows that sometimes a boy like me could earn a few pennies herding them down to graze along the river. Our little town had boasted four taverns. Visitors could stay at the Taylor, Potomac House, or Globe Hotel. Zeller's huge livery stable on East Salisbury Street was always busy, and mail and passenger coaches ran to Pennsylvania and Virginia 'most every day. When I was little I used to squat on the corner, watching the six-horse wagons passing from the coalyards along the canal.

After three years of war, Williamsport was a stinking shadow. More than half our neighbors were gone—run off, or dead. Earlier that year soldiers had brought smallpox to town. Rebel artillery on the Virginia side of the river sent three shells crashing into the Catholic church. Broken windows and leaking roofs went unrepaired. The soldiers forever passing through sometimes ripped down parts of vacant houses or shops, wanting the wood for their campfires. And they stole whatever food and livestock they could find, leaving the gnawed bones lying about with the rest of their waste.

Now, the arrival of the Confederate ambulance train and its escort had swelled the village to bursting. The rain had stopped but the sky had a gray bloated look to it, like it might unleash on us again any minute. The roads were full of Rebels, and I saw some artillery pieces. A few townsfolk were skedaddling out of the way to safer ground, yanking children along or pushing wheelbarrows or dragging heavy carpetbags. But most of the folks afeared of trouble, or with somewhere else to go, had fled Williamsport long ago.

Since the war began our town had changed hands more often than any other town in Maryland, some said. We'd seen armies come and go, endured shelling by Rebels trying to destroy canal traffic, been engulfed by refugees and fugitive slaves running from their masters, fought off stragglers more interested in thieving than fighting, even cleaned up after nearby skirmishing. So we were used to being awash in hard times and fighting and soldiers and such. That day I kept my head low as I'd learned, not looking for any trouble, and headed straight for St. Augustine's Catholic Church on East Potomac Street.

The road in front was clogged with more of those Confederate ambulance wagons, and strings of mules. I waited off to one side while two men carried more wounded Rebels on stretchers into the church. Then, I saw Mrs. Huxley coming out, and waited another minute so I wouldn't have to look at her. The Huxleys were for the Confederacy. Even though Maryland was officially in the Union, with us being right on the border, there was more than a bit of disagreement among folks in town. We'd pretty much learned to pretend the Rebel sympathizers didn't exist, and they gave it right back to us. There was some folks you spoke to on the street, others you didn't.

Among the Confederate-minded souls—we called them Secessionists—the womenfolks were the worst. The men were mostly gone: in the army, or skedaddled, or anyhow too afraid to show their feelings for fear the Unionists would arrest them once the Rebels had moved on. But the women always pinched their cheeks and sashayed forth whenever Rebs were about.

I'd been watching from shore when the Rebel army crossed into Maryland at the end of June. It was raining, which should have been a lesson to them, I was thinking. Someone pointed out General Lee, and two lesser generals named Longstreet and Pickett, riding together with their staff officers following close behind. Some of those clattering Secesh women traipsed down to the riverbank with big umbrellas, waiting to give what they minded was a fitting welcome to Maryland. They insisted on being properly presented, there in the mud and the rain, with the officers looking like they'd rather just keep going toward some place dry.

One woman was determined to place a wreath of flowers around the neck of Longstreet's horse, which the horse objected to mightily, and only after some wrassling on her part did she finally consent to let one of Longstreet's staff officers take it. Another Secesh woman kept asking for a lock of Lee's hair, so loud I heard her clear under the elm tree near the landing where I was watching. He said he had none to spare, but perhaps General Pickett would oblige. That Pickett fellow, I heard later, was famous for his corkscrew ringlets. That day everybody's hair was hanging lank and dripping down their collars, and I never did hear if he gave up any of it for those ladies.

I stood watching under that elm tree, hating those women almost as much as I hated the Rebels for killing my pa and brothers. Those women didn't give up, either. When the generals had moved on they stood there in the rain calling "Welcome to Maryland!" while the foot soldiers sloshed up on shore, even though some of those cursed Rebs had taken their trousers off for the crossing, which caused more than a mite of mortification among the younger ladies in the bunch.

Seeing Mrs. Huxley come out of the church that day reminded me all over again. I should have known her and her ilk would be about, I thought sourly, tending to their heroes. Well, the Yankees were on their way to end the war once and for all. The Secesh folks had cheered their soldiers off to do battle in Pennsylvania, and now they had to bind their wounds 'cause they'd come back beaten and bloody. Stiffed up by the thought, I marched inside.

I wasn't ready for what I saw. What I heard. What I smelled.

The sanctuary was crammed with wounded Rebels: on the pews, in the aisle, up by the altar. I got a quick glimpse of filthy, bloody men. Heard a dull din of voices moaning, groaning, yelling, calling for God and Mother and Emma and Lulie Jo. Orderlies were moving among them, and a few women with baskets on their arms, and a surgeon or two in blood-stained aprons. The place stunk of sweat and blood and feces and burned meat.

Had Pa and the boys been taken to places like this when they'd been hit? Had they died calling for Maureen, for Mother, for Agnes? I leaned against the wall to steady myself. My stomach looked again for something to shove back up. Then a firm hand clamped my arm and dragged me back outside.

"Chigger O'Malley. What're you doing here?" Father Ryan's face swam against the sky. He was a young man, but in the last two years his eyes had grown old. Today, they looked worried and tired and...and something else, all at the same time.

"I came looking for you, Father. I'd consider it a kind favor if you could come out to our place and visit with Ma."

"Is she ill?"

"No, well…," I hesitated. "Some Rebs came this morning and made us take in one of their own. Put him to bed right there. She's taking it hard."

"Your poor mother has carried a weary load. But Chig, I can't be leaving the church just now. I'm needed here, lad."

I wrenched away from him. "You'd be blessing the Rebels before one of your own?"

"There's men dying in there," Father Ryan said softly.

"And there's one dying at my house." The words popped out. Suddenly my knees turned soft and I sank on the steps, staring at the street. Mrs. Huxley had stopped to talk to one of the drivers. I couldn't hear what she said, but the man threw back his head and brayed with laughter. He sounded for all the world like one of his danged mules.

The priest's hand settled on my shoulder. "Chigger, what's weighing on you? Is it concern for a dying Confederate that brought you here?"

I struggled for words, hard when everything inside was so tangled. "Father Ryan," I finally mumbled, "is it murder to kill an enemy soldier?"

He sucked in his breath, seemed to hold it for a long moment before blowing it back out. "Oh, lad. Do you mean on a battlefield?"

I hesitated, trying wildly to decide what to tell him. If I said the truth, would I want to hear his response?

Father Ryan peered at me like he could see straight into my heart. "I don't know that killing's pure murder if done in the midst of a battle. But even on a battlefield, once the shooting stops, a Christian man would bind up another's wounds no matter what color uniform he wore."

I struggled to understand what he was telling me. "But—"

"Father Ryan!" Someone stuck his head out the door. "They're calling for you. That Georgia boy—"

"I'm coming." The priest was on his way at once, black robe fluttering. "Chig, I'll come out when I can," he promised over his shoulder. Then he disappeared.

"Stupid priest," I mumbled, then crossed myself quick. It wasn't the first time I'd come to Father Ryan for help with Ma. It hadn't occurred to me that he might not come.

I scooted over to the edge of the step, out of the way, and considered. I wished like anything I had someone else to turn to. Even just to talk to. But I had no kin left living but Ma. And my friends from before the war were all gone. Jimmy Ryerson's family had packed up and left pretty quick, looking to be out of the armies' path, Mr. Ryerson said. Gerald Dugan and his mother had moved away too, after his pa got killed. And Leonard Tippler's folks had chosen for the Confederacy, and moved across the Potomac to Virginia.

That left only Robert Kincaid—and calling him a friend was a stretch. If he hadn't hired on somewhere, I could probably find him hanging around Charlie Troxell's old blacksmith shop, with one or two of the other men who had no place to go and nothing to do. But they tended to talk more than listen.

It all combined to make me powerful lonesome. I was the only O'Malley man left, and had to take charge. But my first charge was making sure Ma was all right, making sure she didn't give in to her grief and just...just shut down altogether. And I didn't have even a muddy idea of how to do that.

After feeling sorry for myself for a few minutes, I screwed up the backbone to head home and see if Tallard was dead yet, and if Ma was still collapsed on the floor. But just as I was about to get up I heard something from the doorway behind me that made me freeze.

"Poor cusses." A man standing just inside the church muttered an oath. "I tell you, Nate, I'd rather take a bullet through the brain than get shot up bad and left behind in some hospital."

"General Imboden's not figurin' on leaving any behind, if he can help it."

"The point is, what he *is* figurin' to do is put all us wagoners out to meet the Yank cavalry. Coop just told me he heard that with his own ears. I signed on to manhandle mules, not fight Yanks."

From behind me came the scrape of a match, a sudden twist of tobacco smoke as someone lit a cigar. I sat rock-still, trying not to be noticed.

"It's a bad scrape," the man named Nate agreed, sounding grim. "But Imboden doesn't have much choice, I guess. Word is that three thousand Yank riders are headed this way. Imboden's got what, maybe two thousand men? Coop said those Yank riders could be here by midday. If we don't hold 'em off somehow—"

"Hey!"

I jumped like lard dropped in a hot skillet when one of the drivers on the street bellowed in my direction. "Nate! Clinch! These busted-up boys ain't going to get in that church by themselves! Quit yer flapping and git back to work!"

He was hollering at the two men behind me. A cigar stub hurtled past toward the curb, and one man mumbled another curse, before they jogged down the steps. Nate got in an argument with the man doing all the yelling, but I watched without really hearing or seeing. My mind was too full of what I'd just heard.

The Yankees were on their way!

It was what I'd been waiting for. The Yankee army, getting ready to pounce. They'd scoop up the wounded in Williamsport, then block the escape route across the Potomac for the rest of the Rebels trudging down from Gettysburg. Neat as pie.

I felt half excited and half sick-shivery again. I thought of Ma, of Tallard, of Father Ryan's troubled eyes. Maybe I shouldn't have been so quick to cause Tallard to bleed to death. Maybe I should have waited, trusted in the Yankee army to take care of their own business. Maybe there *was* a difference between killing the enemy in battle and killing him while he lay helpless in bed.

Maybe I *was* a murderer.

I had to wait while Nate and Clinch hauled another stretcher up the stairs and into the church. Then I tumbled down the steps and headed for home.

CHAPTER FIVE

JULY 6, 1863

The clouds split as I was leaving the church, and I ran home in another hard-driving rain. When I burst soaked and dripping through the door, the first thing I saw was that Rebel Sergeant Krick leaning over the bed. My heart about fell out of my chest. When he glared at me I froze like an icicle hanging from the eaves, waiting for the shot that would blow my head off. *Oh Ma, I did you poorly—*

Then Krick turned back to the corpse in the bed. "So anyway, we got the rest of the boys settled on up the road." And the corpse smiled weakly, nodded. "How's Michael Tipton?" Tallard asked, clear enough for me to hear across the room.

Tallard wasn't dead.

After I took that in, I got pulled toward the bed as if by an invisible string. The pillow was back on the bed. Tallard's arm was resting on it. And George Tallard was very much alive.

"He's bedded down in an old German couple's stable, a mile or so down," Krick was saying. "I found him a nice dry pile of straw."

Tallard nodded, but his gaze slowly moved up to catch mine. I felt my own eyes grow wider still, and I took a step backwards. Waited for Tallard's remaining arm to rise, to point at me. Waited for him to say, "*That boy tried to kill me...*"

But instead, "He'll mend quicker now he's got a place to rest," he said, and let his look shift back to Krick. "My boys, Sergeant. You've got to look after all the boys in the company. Promise me that. God knows there aren't many left."

"I will." Krick sounded like he was soothing a child. "I will, and so will the other sergeants. Don't worry so."

"And the letter? The letter about Louis? They deserve the truth." Tallard was gripping the sergeant's arm so hard his knuckles were white.

"I've got it, tucked away safe. Soon as we're across the Potomac I'll make sure it's delivered. You got my word. I already told you that." Krick gently pulled away, then straightened. "Look, Captain, I can't stay."

Tallard sagged back against the pillow and closed his eyes. "Of course."

"I'll be back for you, when I can. You need to rest until General Imboden figures out how to get the wagon train back across the Potomac. River's already falling."

"Do something for me?" Tallard fumbled at his side. "In my pocket...I can't quite..."

Krick rummaged for him, then pulled out a tintype. A bolt of lightning shot through my insides. It had the same brass frame, all flags and eagles and such, as the images on our mantle.

Tallard curled his fingers around it, so I didn't see the actual likeness. He looked content. "I'm beholden."

Krick took a few steps toward the kitchen. "Woman!"

Ma appeared in the doorway, arms folded, eyes narrow. "Where's that coffee?"

I realized I smelled coffee, an almost-forgotten memory. Ma disappeared into the kitchen, and returned with a steaming tin mug. She smacked it on the table so hard some of the brew sloshed over the rim. Then she stalked back into the kitchen.

Krick jerked around and pointed at me. "Boy. Let that cool, then make sure he drinks as much as he wants. You hear?"

I nodded dumbly, wondering how he'd gotten that horrible bruise on his cheek. Wondering how many Yankees he'd killed. Wondering why he was leaving me to tend Tallard. Was it a trap? Maybe Tallard *had* told him, and—

There was no knowing. Without so much as a by-your-leave, Krick walked out.

I stood like a scarecrow for a moment, my insides all a-churn again. I'd run all the way from Williamsport feeling more and more a murderer with every step. Now here was Tallard alive, and Krick still ordering me about in my own home! It was beyond tolerable. The guilt I'd felt creeping in was gone, replaced again with the old anger, and a sense of failure.

Lord Almighty, it was confusing. I'd felt bad when I thought I'd killed Tallard, and felt just as bad when I found that I hadn't!

All that jumble of feelings popped out angry and mean. "Yankee cavalry's coming," I blurted. "I heard so in town. Three thousand riders, with the rest of the Union army coming along behind."

"I expect they are."

"And that Sergeant Krick was lying. The river's still high. There's a big battle coming, and the Yankees are going to come down and kill you all."

"Maybe so."

I didn't know what to say to that. Silence cloaked the room. I looked at the mug of coffee. I was angry enough again to ignore Krick's order to me. But Tallard wasn't likely to die because I didn't give him a cup of coffee. Besides...hadn't I decided it was best to leave the actual killing to the armies? The Yankee army would be here soon enough.

When I fetched the cup I noticed that the coffee was full of grounds. Ma had boiled that coffee to make it bitter, and not added the usual dash of cold water to settle the grounds. I felt my mouth twitch toward a smile, as forgotten as the smell of coffee. These rare moments, when Ma roused herself to keep fighting, gave me hope.

Tallard tried to raise his head from the pillow. It was hard, him with one arm and all, and my free hand went out to support his left shoulder. I'd never touched a Rebel before. I was aware of every fiber in his filthy shirt, a clot of mud, the stiffness of dried blood. It set me to shaking, and made me want to wash my hands. I don't know that Tallard got more than a gulp of coffee because I spilled half of it down his chin.

He used his good arm to wipe it off. "Thank you."

Infernal Rebel! "What are you thanking me for?" I asked crossly, wiping my hands hard on my trousers.

"The coffee."

I didn't understand this Rebel, sure as you're born. "Why didn't you tell on me?"

Soon as the words were out of my mouth I wanted to snatch them back. But Tallard didn't answer. Instead he turned his head, waved his hand toward the fireplace, where the four black-draped tintypes marched across the mantelpiece. "Who are they?"

The cabin was so still I heard the rain pounding outside, and a rumble of thunder. I wondered if Ma was listening from the kitchen. "My pa and my three older brothers." The words dropped like chips of ice. "They're all dead. You...you *Rebels* killed them all."

I don't know if he would have answered. Instead, I heard the first pepper of gunfire in the distance. Hang the Rebel. I didn't have time for him now. "Ma!" I hollered, and bolted to the kitchen.

She was sitting still as stone, staring at the wall. At least she was on a chair this time, not the floor. I grabbed her arm. "Ma, come on. There's shooting outside." She let me tug her up, into the main room. I glanced back at the bed before we headed out. Tallard was watching me. I pulled Ma's arm again and we ran outside.

I heard more thunder as I towed Ma through the muck to the little root cellar that Pa had years ago dug into the hillside behind the house, and realized it was artillery making this storm, not the heavens. Once inside the root cellar I pulled the door shut behind us best I could. It only latched from the outside. Pa hadn't figured on anyone wanting to be latched *inside* the root cellar.

There was just a narrow aisle between two short rows of shelves where in good times we'd stored potatoes, apples, turnips—all the things a body needs to get through the winter. Now the shelves were empty. Ma sank to the ground between them, drew up her knees, buried her face in her arms.

I tried to shore her up. "It's the Yankees, Ma. They're coming to liberate Williamsport. They're coming to destroy the Rebels and end the war. I figure they'll deal with these wounded men first, then guard the ford and swallow up the rest of the Rebel army."

She didn't answer. After a moment I sat down too, and leaned against a shelf. I could feel the cold damp seeping through the heavy stuff of my trousers. I should have thought to bring stools.

It wasn't the first time we'd sought shelter here. When a Rebel force crossed the Potomac a few miles south of Williamsport at Falling Waters in 1861, there'd been a battle on the Maryland side. It was a puny one, compared to what was to come after, but at the time we'd heard the shooting and taken cover. Then four of us had squeezed in here, me and Ma and Patrick and Liam. Pa and Egan were already gone.

Later, after Patrick left home, it had been me and Ma and Liam when there was more shooting, small skirmishes that broke out like brush fires whenever some Rebels crossed the river to make trouble. I'd seen Rebel riders pound down our road with Yankee cavalry chasing close behind, every one shooting and hollering. I'd dug lead balls from the logs of our house with my pocketknife, and once helped pick up broken glass where one had come through the kitchen window.

Now it was just me and Ma. Would she huddle in the root cellar alone one day, when trouble came and I was off to war in the footsteps of my father and brothers? Or would she sit in the house if I wasn't there to drag her to safety?

I reminded myself that I needn't ask that question. Once the Yankees beat the Rebels this last time, right here in Williamsport, the war would surely end. The other pieces of the great armies, the ones fighting in the west, would surely give in too if the mighty Confederate General Robert E. Lee was defeated for good. When that happened, I wouldn't have to figure out if my path lay in taking care of my mother or avenging the slain O'Malley men. I'd stay home, and try to build up what we had. And maybe Ma would even one day take the fiddle down from the wall and play...

My stomach's rumble interrupted that daydream. I still hadn't eaten that day. Odd, how the root cellar still smelled of parsnips and such, even though there had been no garden to harvest that year. Odder still, I found myself wondering about that cursed Rebel Tallard, lying alone in our cabin, hearing the firing come closer. Was he thinking about being hungry too? Or was he looking at the ceiling, wondering when some Yankee cannonball might crash through and kill him once and for all?

Today, I thought in wonder. The war could end today.

CHAPTER SIX

JULY 6, 1863

The war didn't end that day. We heard gunfire off and on 'til night slipped across the landscape. I was hollow as a bee gum by then, and not caring a whit about it if only the soldiers I saw after opening that root cellar door were wearing Yankee blue.

They weren't.

That Rebel General Imboden fellow, so we heard later, had deployed his men out to meet the Yankee threat. That included sending out some seven hundred wagoners, commanded by wounded officers hobbling about and shouting orders with arms in slings and bloody bandages wrapped around their heads. They even hauled out some of the wounded, and sat them against trees, and put guns in their hands. Somehow that ragtag force managed, in the pouring rain, to hold off our Yankees until nightfall, when a Confederate cavalry leader arrived from the northeast with about three thousand of his own Rebel riders. Word came that more Rebel horsemen were pounding down another road. The Yankee troops we'd been so counting on broke off their attack and withdrew to the southeast, away from our place. That brawl came to be known as the Wagoner's Fight.

I didn't know all the details that night. All I knew was that when the shooting stopped, and Ma and I walked down our lane to see what was what, the soldiers splashing by on the main road were more of the cursed Rebels. One of the riders slogging past in the gloom laughed about "sending those Yanks skedaddling."

Ma turned on me. "Chigger, where are the Yankees?" she hissed. Her claws bit into my shoulder and jerked me around. "You said the Yankees were coming, Chig! You said!"

"I thought they were, Ma," I managed. She had a lot of strength left in those fiddling fingers. "Maybe tomorrow. We'll have to wait."

I stuffed my disappointment into the hollow place where breakfast, lunch, and dinner should have been. We went back inside and found Tallard still alive. A shell hadn't come through the roof and killed him where he lay. He didn't say anything, just watched us come in and light a lamp.

Neither of us could abide sitting with him. Ma stirred herself to mix up some biscuits with the Rebel flour, and we had a sorry meal long after dark. I took a couple in to Tallard, and a cup of water. He put his tintype on the bed while he struggled with the biscuits, and I got a glimpse of his family. A mournful-looking woman and two big-eyed children, a boy and a girl, stared at the camera.

Somehow, that quick peek just stoked up the anger smoldering inside. Those children still had a father. Mine was dead. And one of the very Rebels who'd killed him was lying in my pa's own bed, in his own home.

"Thank you," Tallard said, holding out the empty cup.

I snatched it from him. "The Yankees are still out there," I told him. "Waiting. Biding their time. Lining up their guns. A shell could come sailing through the roof any minute and land right on top of you." Would Tallard end up in pieces, like Liam? Sliced up in pieces so his family didn't even have a body to bury?

Tallard just nodded, and I turned away, the flame already burned back down to coals. I was suddenly too tired, too discouraged, to get in more of a fret with him.

When my brothers were alive we'd slept in the stable loft through all but the coldest nights. Lately I'd been bedding down in the corner across from Ma. With Tallard there, Ma and I slept in the kitchen. When I curled up on a blanket under the kitchen table, Ma was still sitting against the wall. "Come lie and rest, Ma," I urged.

"You're all I got, Chig," she said, like she hadn't heard. "Promise me you won't go off to war."

"I won't go. But you need to get some sleep."

She didn't heed. I can't say I slept easy either. I kept hearing the words I'd said to Tallard. Trying to imagine what would happen if the shell I was looking for *did* crash through the ceiling and blow him to bits.

And against my will, those big hound dog-eyed children in his tintype picture kept floating through my dreams, staring at me. I felt guilty for wishing their father ripped to pieces with an artillery shell. Then I saw my pa's eyes staring, and Egan's and Patrick's and Liam's, and I felt guilty for *regretting* that I'd wished Tallard dead.

With such troubled sleep, I jerked awake when Ma touched my shoulder. The night was still full, and black as tar. I heard muttering from the main room. It came fretful at first. Impossible to make out. Then a low moan brought goose bumps to my skin.

"Something's wrong with the Rebel," Ma whispered.

I didn't want to move. Something about those noises coming out of the dark gave me the shakes. I had to remind myself good and proper that I was Ma's only protection, now. "I'll see to it," I finally whispered back.

It seemed an eternity before I'd found matches and got a lamp lit. We hadn't been using lamps for a while, since oil was so dear, and I managed to snuff the light the first time I tried to adjust the wick. Finally, the lamp was lit and the glass chimney in place. In the shadows I saw Ma sitting on the floor with her knees drawn up tight, her eyes wide. "Stay here," I whispered.

I crept into the next room and raised the lamp. Tallard was still muttering, stringing odd words together. "Louis...advance...I didn't know!...Have to tell Mary about Louis..." From across the room I could see his head turning back and forth on the pillow.

"Hey! Tallard!" My voice cracked like a musket shot through the room.

If he heard me he didn't let on. I crept closer. The night air was damp and heavy. I felt a trickle of sweat run down my back.

Tallard was twitching like a new-butchered chicken. "Forward double quick...the surgeon. Have to call the surgeon...it's Louis..."

I didn't know what to do. "Tallard!" I called again, real sharp. I held the lamp high and saw that his eyes were open. Staring, but not seeing anything in the room. Those glassy eyes gave me the spooks all over again.

"What's the matter with him?" Ma was standing in the doorway behind me.

"He's either fevered or...or having a nightmare." I couldn't tell. I remembered Ma touching my forehead when I was a child, to see if I had a fever. Reluctantly I stretched out one hand, took a deep breath, and pressed my fingers against the Reb's forehead. It was warm and damp, and I snatched my hand back like I'd been burned. "Louis, don't," Tallard mumbled.

"I don't think he's got a bad fever," I told Ma. "But I can't tell for sure."

"Come back to bed. There's nothing to do for him anyway."

I was glad enough to turn my back on the Rebel. But long after I'd curled back on the blanket in the kitchen I lay awake, listening to Tallard toss and moan. It was a long night.

CHAPTER SEVEN

JULY 7, 1863

The next morning, Tallard seemed no worse off than the day before. I gave him a good look as I fetched his night-jar to empty outside, but his shakes and mumbles were done with. I was curious, but not enough to make conversation with the man. So I left him be.

I waited to hear the opening guns as the Yankees pushed in again, harder this time, to capture the Rebels. Waited, and waited, and waited. Finally I had to get out of the house. Tallard's staring eyes, Ma's silence, marched across my skin like ants. It was enough to make me go mad. I checked the stable, looking for company, but there was no sign of Robert beyond a hollowed-out place in the straw. So I walked in to Williamsport. Walked, and walked, and walked.

There was a lot to see and I didn't like any of it. That Rebel General Longstreet's infantry tramped into town that morning, footsore and mud-caked and looking like whipped dogs. And more columns came behind them, miles and miles of infantry, all bottling up around town. Soon we were as flooded with Rebels as we had been with rain. There was no place for them to go, so they piled up like flotsam against the shore. They took over cabins and churches and pigsties, slept like cordwood in muddy farmyards, rigged tiny shelters among the trees.

At the same time, more Rebel soldiers were digging into a defensive line. They formed an arc, generally facing east around Williamsport. The left of their line was near the mouth of the Conococheague, close by where Agnes and baby Willis lived. The right end was south of town, across the Potomac from Falling Waters, Virginia. I climbed up Cemetery Hill and saw those Rebels forming an impressive fortification, like a fence built of earth. For skinny, whipped boys they sure could dig.

In the cemetery, a few lanky Rebels were digging graves for the dead killed in the Wagoner's Fight. The same sacred hill where my pa and Egan and Patrick lay! The sight burned inside me but I didn't know what to do about it. I turned away from the burial party and looked east, beyond the farmers' wet-gold wheat fields outside town.

Where in tarnation were the Yankees?

I didn't notice one of the Rebels come up behind me until he spoke. "They're all out there somewhere," he laughed, waving his arm. "Two armies. They say Yankee cavalry is holding the mountain passes, guarding the approaches so the army can advance. But they're moving like molasses. Our boys are digging in six feet deep." He pointed at the trenches and earthen walls ringing Williamsport, tiny in the distance. "And *our* cavalry's protecting the rest of our infantry while they tramp south. If the Yanks come, we'll be ready for 'em. We're itchin' for another fight."

I marched away without a word, but slipped and landed on my backside as I tried to retreat down the hill. I heard the Rebel laughing above me, and wanted to take a stick to him. I didn't know who I was angrier at, the Rebels for being so ornery or the Yankees for being so slow. Even I could see that every minute that passed gave the Rebels more time to dig in and prepare for a big fight.

General Lee had also set some of his men to work on a new pontoon bridge. Rebels were ranging about for lumber,

"General Lee's army crossing the Potomac at Williamsport, in scows guided by wires." As the Yankee army approached, the Confederates worked frantically to ferry troops across the flood-swollen Potomac River.

Frank Leslie's *Illustrated*, August 1863; courtesy Frank & Marie-Therese Wood Print Collection, Alexandria, Virginia.

tearing down abandoned houses and the like, hauling or floating it downstream toward Falling Waters. Worse, I found a bustle of activity down by the Williamsport ford. Some cursed Rebel had scrounged up a couple of small flatboats, and they'd somehow managed to rig a line across the Potomac. By the time I wandered down for a look-see they were already carrying wounded down, packing them on the flatboats, and ferrying them across.

Now mind, they could only get about 30 wounded men across at a time, and I'd heard there were more than 10,000 hurt Rebels in Williamsport. It wasn't like they were gushing across to safety. More like a trickle. But even that trickle worried me. I didn't want any of 'em to escape. On top of that, the ferryboats coming back from the Virginia side were loaded with crates. By the way the Rebs whooped and hollered when they unloaded them, I figured they were being supplied with ammunition.

After watching that dismal sight for a spell I wandered up Clear Spring Road to look in on Agnes and baby Willis. I didn't know if her folks were back yet or not. As I walked up the hill I saw two Rebels come out the front door of Agnes's house, bold as brass and clatter down the steps. After that I didn't bother knocking, just walked inside myself. "Agnes?"

I found her in the kitchen frying up griddle cakes, looking hot and bothered. Willis was gurgling in a cradle in the corner. "Oh, Chigger," she said when she looked up and saw me. "I figured you for another Rebel."

"I saw two leaving just now. Wanted to make sure you're well."

Agnes pushed a strand of damp hair back from her forehead. "They forced some wounded on me. Eight of 'em, although one died this morning. I've had to cook for 'em all. And I've got a mountain of laundry. I feel like spittin' in every one's eye. But I can't say they've made any real trouble."

"We've got one at our place too."

"I guess everybody has at least one or two." Agnes flipped several griddle cakes onto a waiting platter. Her family had always been better off than mine, and they still had such things left: stoneware platters and china teacups.

"Are your folks back yet?"

"No. I don't think they could get through the lines, now that the armies are here. I heard from one of the men this morning that there's skirmishing going on north and east of here." She paused to pour more batter on the hot griddle. "I hope my parents are somewhere safe. I don't want them on the road now."

"I'm sure they're well," I said, wanting to buck her up. "But Agnes…I don't know that you should be staying here alone, with all these Rebs in the house."

"I'm all right. They left one bedroom for me and the baby. I lock myself in at night."

"It's not safe," I said stubbornly, although I didn't have an idea in the world of what I could do for her. There was less to offer at our place than here, that was certain. "The Yankees could break through any time. Shells could come this way any minute. I'm expecting a big fight."

"Maybe there won't be a battle. From what I'm hearing, the bulk of the Yankee army isn't close yet. Just an advance guard, trying to keep the Rebels busy. Once the rest of the Yankees get here, they can overpower the Rebels—"

"If the Rebels don't get across the Potomac first," I reminded her grimly.

"Yes. If they don't get across the Potomac first."

"They're working on it." I told her about the flatboat ferry I'd seen, and the plans to string together a new pontoon bridge. "But the river's still too high to ford an army on foot. If the Yankees just get here in time, they can kill the lot of 'em."

"They wouldn't kill all the wounded," Agnes said. She opened the firebox door on the stove with her apron, then shoved in another stick of wood. "They'd just capture them, I think."

I considered. My imaginings hadn't wasted much time on prisoners. It was dead Rebels I'd been dreaming of, not captured ones. "What would they do with 'em all? There's ten thousand wounded."

Agnes shrugged. "I heard twelve thousand. The Yankees would send the lot of them off to prison camps, I guess."

Prison camps. Maybe that was the answer, especially where Tallard was concerned. I'd failed in my attempt to kill him, and been tormented by my wish that the Yankees blow him to bits for me. But I could wish Tallard in prison, couldn't I? Maybe sitting around some prison camp with nothing to do but face his nightmares was fair punishment for what he and his kind had done. Maybe I could even find a way to help make it possible. When the Yankees came I could run out to meet them, point them toward our little lane. "In that cabin," I'd say. "There's one more Rebel in there." And some Yankee general with gold braid on his sleeves would say, "Thanks, lad. We might have missed him."

A slammed door, a shouted curse, reminded me that things might not be so tidy, even when the entire Yankee army did arrive. "Agnes, maybe you should take Willis and go stay somewhere. With one of the ladies from your church. Wait 'til everything calms down."

"I could never leave, Chig. They'd clean the house out sure as you're born. As long as I stay, and do their cooking and cleaning and such, they won't hurt me."

"I wish your folks were back."

"It wouldn't change anything. As soon as Father comes back he'll be kept busy with the wounded. And Mother's not good for much in the face of trouble. I can manage."

"It's just not right," I grumbled. I hated feeling so helpless. I was Willis's best protector. But what could I do? Helplessness, anger, balled hard and sour in my belly.

Suddenly she smiled a little. It went into her eyes, and she was pretty in a way I'd never seen before. She let her hand rest on my shoulder for a moment. "You're sweet, Chigger," she said softly. "You mind me some of Liam. I sure miss him."

"I miss him too," I mumbled, but my mind was turning on her first words. "Do you really think I'm like him?"

"A bit." She smiled again, then began flipping those griddle cakes.

I thought that over. All my life I'd been the youngest O'Malley, little more than a pesky fly to my older brothers. Now that they were all gone, I had to fill all their boots and Pa's too. It was too much, I tell you, too much. But no one had ever told me I reminded them of *any* of the other O'Malley men. It heartened me considerable to hear Agnes say so.

"Agnes...what was he like with you?"

She looked startled. "What do you mean?"

I felt my face grow hot. I hadn't meant to be impertinent. "I just meant, he was a good brother to me, but looking back I feel like I never really knew him. Not as...as himself. Just as a brother." I was making a mess of it. How could I explain that there was a time I'd thought I knew Liam inside and out...but then he married this Methodist girl, and marched off to war soon after, without ever explaining why. And before I could figure any of it out, he was dead.

Agnes tipped her head to one side, considering. "He was thoughtful. And gentle. And a good listener. A real good listener." Her eyes were suddenly shining, like she was real close to crying. "I'll tell you what, Chig. I thank God every day that I have Willis. A little bit of Liam still here, to keep going. I don't know that I could get out of bed in the morning if I didn't have Willis." One tear brimmed over and rolled down her cheek.

Now I'd done it! I'd made Agnes cry. I wasn't good for anything, that was sure. I wanted like anything to run out, but it seemed too rude, what with her upset and all. Instead I crammed my hands in my pockets and walked over to stare down at Willis.

He didn't look like much, but then, I didn't know anything about babies. He didn't have any hair. I looked at his face and tried to see Liam, and came up short. Still, what Agnes said stuck with me. A little bit of Liam still here...I suddenly wished Patrick and Egan had married and fathered too, even if they'd done it with Protestant girls from families with more money than ours.

"You want to hold him?"

I shook my head. "Naw—"

"Oh, here." After pulling the griddle to a cooler spot on the stove, she scooped up Willis and plunked him in my arms. "Watch his head, now. Always keep a hand under his head."

Willis made a face and wiggled like bait, then settled back down. He was a pint-sized mite of a thing. I stared down at the tiny face, wee fingers. Liam's son! It seemed a miracle.

I was suddenly sure I'd drop him on his head, and gave him back. "Listen, Agnes. I gotta get going. I just stopped in to make sure they weren't treating you too bad."

She kissed Willis's head and tucked him back in the cradle. "I'm holding up," she said stoutly. "And Chigger? Tell your mother she's welcome any time, if she wants to see Willis. Really."

That was kind. Like I said before, there wasn't any bad blood between Agnes's family and mine. We just didn't mix much, especially now that Liam was dead. "I'll tell her." I watched Agnes get back to her cooking, then turned to go.

"Chig!"

When I looked back she jerked her wrist and one-two-three hot griddle cakes sailed through the air. "Rebel breakfast," she said, with a little grin. "They'll never miss 'em."

I stuffed down those cakes before I reached Agnes's front steps—before any thieving Rebel could see me and steal 'em, or take Agnes to task. They warmed my belly and my heart. I was beginning to understand what Liam had seen in Agnes.

CHAPTER EIGHT

JULY 8, 1863

That night it rained again. A fierce, hard, cold rain. I lay on the kitchen floor picturing all those Rebels digging fortifications, ferrying the flatboats across the Potomac, and working on the pontoon bridge. I hoped every scrap of their labors got washed away.

By morning the storm had slid off to a light misting rain. It was quiet. Too quiet, meaning I didn't hear any guns signaling the fight that would end the war. "I'll walk you through town if you like, Ma," I told her. "Agnes said you could come any time, and see Willis. You'd probably be a help."

"Agnes has her own women to help her tend the child." Ma was beating up more biscuits with the Rebel flour, and she took the spoon to the dough like it was a Rebel backside.

"Her folks aren't back yet. I'm sure she'd be pleased, what with her own mama gone and all."

"Chig, I'm not going into town when it's full of Rebels! It's bad enough I got one here."

"Maybe you could take the fiddle, and play a lullaby..."

For a moment I thought she might take the spoon to me. I couldn't find the words to say that Willis had come into the world without a father, and there was nothing better to ease him into this troubled life than one of her lullabies.

Instead I retreated outside, cursing myself for bungling another attempt to cheer up Ma. After a moment of thought I slogged back through the mud to check our three cherry trees. At this time of year we should have been feasting on cherries, but soldiers cutting through stole every one as soon as it looked even half-ripe. Still, it was worth checking. If even a few had escaped notice, they'd be a real treat for Ma.

I started to feel a mite better. Surely the rain had undone all the Rebels' work. Maybe they'd even give up, just surrender, and all get shipped off to prison camps… Maybe Ma would rosin her bow if peace was declared.

I even found a handful of cherries.

Then I heard a shout from the front. I crammed the fruit in my pocket and slip-slided around the house. An old farm wagon was sitting in the drive, hitched to two ancient mules. One Rebel was holding the lines. Two more were headed for our front door.

"Hey!" I shouted. I wanted to head 'em off before they got to Ma.

The Rebels stopped and waited. "This your place?" one asked. He was skinny as a sapling and too young to shave, I'd guess. Dark hair hung lank and damp past his ears.

"Yes. And we don't have any livestock left. Or food—"

"We ain't here for food." He gestured toward the wagon. It was piled with kettles, a bucket or two, even a few washbasins. "You see—"

"Oh for the love of Jesus," the second man interrupted. He was just as skinny, just as young, just as dirty. "You don't have to explain yourself to these people, Tully. They'd stick a knife in your ribs soon as you're born—"

"We come for a kettle," Tully announced firmly, waving his friend to silence. "We're boiling tar, y'see. To plug up the boats—"

"Tully!" The second man sounded exasperated. "These people are Yanks!"

"You don't know that, Jim!" Tully snapped. "Some of 'em around these parts are for us. Captain said we had to be polite. No way of knowing who's who…"

While they argued my new hopes sank like a rock tossed into the Potomac. Boiling tar to patch boats! That meant the Rebels were going ahead with their plans to try to get across the river before the Yankees scooped them up. I should have known they'd never just sit and surrender, rain or no rain. They were still trying to escape.

Well, they wouldn't get my help. "We don't have a kettle."

That brought them both around. "Sure you do," Tully said finally.

"You boys have been here before. Stolen everything we have."

"A bucket, then. A washtub."

I crossed my arms over my chest. "Nope. Nothing."

Jim shoved by Tully, rifle in hand. "You don't mind that we check the house then, do you, boy? You see, it's up to you. You give us a kettle, or we tear your place apart looking for one."

For a moment I was tempted. I hated giving in to 'em. But what would I win by letting them tear apart our place? Nothing. And I could lose a lot.

"You wait here." I spat the words like cherry pits on the ground.

"Nothing tin," Jim called after me. "Nothing that won't hold up to heat. We want iron."

Ma had heard the commotion and was waiting inside with folded arms and pinched lips. "They need a kettle," I told her. "If we don't give it over, they'll come in and take it."

"We've only got the one," Ma said slowly.

I knew it was true. All our buckets but a little tin pail had already been stolen. So had the big outdoor copper kettle used for soap making and laundry boiling and apple butter cooking. Our kitchen washbasin and coffeepot were made of tin. All we had left that would suit their purpose was one iron kettle. When food was to be had, Ma used that kettle every day.

"We don't have a choice," I told her. "You stay inside. I'll take care of it."

I glared at Tallard as I passed through the main room. Once outside, I dropped the kettle at the Rebels' feet. "It's all we got," I told them. "And one of your own wounded men is inside. Don't blame us if we can't cook proper for him."

"You'll tend him proper or be sorry," Jim said. He picked up the kettle and headed for the wagon.

"I'm sorry to bring more trouble," Tully said more quietly, before following. I felt the old helpless frustration boil inside of me, wishing like anything I had something to do besides watch them steal from us again.

But I hadn't counted on Ma. All of a sudden she blazed out the door like a woman on fire. An armload of kitchen fixings clattered to the ground. "You want to steal from us?" she hollered. *"Here!"* She heaved her frying pan after the retreating Rebs. It caught Tully square between the shoulders. "And *here!*" The coffeepot hurtled toward the wagon, spooking the mules. "And *here! And here!*" A spoon. The washbasin. "And *here!*" A tin cup.

The cup caught Jim in the chest, 'cause by that time he was charging back through the mud like an angry bull.

I tore past Ma to meet him, knowing only that I needed to put myself in the middle. Jim raised an arm and swatted me aside like a fly. For all that he was skin and bones he packed a wallop. I went flying and landed in the mud so hard the world spun around. An iron band was forged around my chest. I couldn't draw breath.

The sounds behind me pulled me back. I painfully pushed up, spitting mud, still gasping for breath, and saw Ma light into the Rebel. He was almost twice her height but for a good moment she held her own, all a blur of flailing arms, pounding fists, and kicking heels. If I'm not mistaken she got in a fierce knee to his gut, for he let out an angry yelp. But he finally managed to grab both her arms.

"Don't hurt her, Jim." But Tully's voice was uncertain, and he didn't make a move to stop the brawl.

Jim ignored him. "Yankee witch!" he panted, lifting Ma clear off the ground. She spat in his face. He began to shake her like rag doll.

I was trying to move but felt like I was caught in a trap, still dizzy and sucking for air. She'd surely gone too far this time. *Oh Ma...*

Then another voice cut across the yard. "Put her down."

We all turned and gaped at the sight of Tallard. The wounded Rebel was leaning against the doorframe, unholy pale and sweating like nobody's business. But he was on his feet.

For a moment the only sound came from me and Ma and Jim, all heaving for breath. Jim lowered Ma to the ground, although he didn't let go of her. "Go back to bed," he told Tallard scornfully. "You must've lost your backbone with that arm."

Tallard managed to push away from the doorframe and stand straight. "I may have lost an arm. But I am still a captain in the Confederate army, *Private.*" The last word seemed a curse. "When I give an order you *will* obey it. Now let go of that woman, get back on your wagon, and leave."

I thought for a moment that Jim wasn't going to obey. Finally, he shoved Ma away and spat on the ground. He sauntered to the wagon with as much bravado as the sucking mud allowed, and tossed our kettle in the bed before climbing to the seat. Tully followed.

Ma sank to her knees, all the fight flowing out of her like cider from the bunghole of a barrel. By the time I'd staggered to her side she'd sagged over, face in her hands.

"Did he hurt you, Ma?" I asked. "Are you all right?"

She didn't answer, but let me pull her gently up and lead her inside. Tallard stepped back from the doorway to let us pass. I noticed the new bright fever spots in his cheeks, and the way he staggered painfully back to the bed, but didn't stop until I'd gotten Ma parked safely on a chair in the kitchen. By the time I passed through the main room again Tallard was lying across the bed, both feet still on the floor like he didn't have enough strength left to lift them.

I went back outside and gathered up our kitchen pieces from the mud where Ma had heaved them, afraid some other thieving Rebels would pass through and clean up for me. When I came back inside I looked at the fiddle hanging on the wall. Thank the Lord she hadn't pitched that too. I couldn't have borne it.

Then I made Ma a cup of tea. "Thank you, Chig," she managed, as I set the steaming mug in front of her. "You're a good boy. You're all I've got left, you know."

"I know Ma." I hesitated, trying to figure how much to say. I didn't blame Ma for what she'd done—I was proud of it, to tell the truth—but I was afraid for her sake. "But you're all I've got left too, you know. You can't go pitching into Rebels like that. You'll get yourself hurt. Or killed."

"We Irish are fighters," she whispered. But she didn't look like much of a fighter anymore, hunched into an old shawl I'd wrapped around her shoulders. I could tell she was disappearing into that place she went in her mind sometimes. Nothing I could say would get through. Sighing, I tucked the shawl a little more firmly around her shoulders and went back into the main room to face Tallard.

His breathing was still labored, his cheeks still flushed. I wondered how much he'd suffered by coming to our aid. Part of me was obliged to him for helping Ma. Part of me held him accountable for all the trouble and grief, and wanted to lash out at him. It was a harsh feeling, like a skirmish was going on inside my chest.

He must have felt me staring at him, for he opened his eyes. "Is your mother well?" he muttered.

"Yes," I said shortly. Then everything tumbled out in a rush. "I'm obliged for what you did. But we wouldn't have been in such a spot if your cursed army hadn't come across the Potomac."

"I suppose not."

"And I heard in town yesterday afternoon that the Yankees are getting close. They may not send a cannonball through the ceiling to land in that bed. But they'll capture every Rebel they can get their hands on and send them off to prison camp. They'll send *you* off to a prison camp."

By the time I was finished speaking my chest was heaving like I'd been running, and my hands were clenched into fists. I was suddenly afraid that if Tallard politely agreed again I'd pitch into him the way Ma had pitched into Jim.

But instead he waved his fingers toward a nearby chair. "Will you sit for a minute?"

I don't know why I did it, but I did.

"What do they call you, boy?"

The unexpected question made me blink. "Chigger."

"Why do they call you that?"

A wash of memories came roaring back like the Potomac in flood. I'd been called Chigger, or Chig, for as long as I could remember. I remembered the day I'd somehow figured out it wasn't a name proper, and had gone to my brothers to ask why everyone called me the name of a tiny insect.

"Because you're so annoying," Egan had laughed.

"Because you're so puny," Patrick echoed.

"Because Ma won't let us call you Woodtick," Liam added.

I was used to my brothers' teasing but this joke had sent me sniveling in to Ma. "Oh, well now. You were indeed a tiny wee babe," she told me. "I was so afeared I'd lose you. 'No bigger than a chigger,' someone said, back when we didn't know if you'd live to outgrow the cradle, and it stuck. But it's a wondrous thing to have such a name. It reminds me how close we came to losing you, and how precious you are to me. I've already got four O'Malley men looking down on me. I don't need another." Somehow, the feel of her fingers smoothing my hair had made me feel like it was a fine enough name after all. I was the only O'Malley boy who didn't tower over Ma, and I hated being runty. But Ma made it seem all right.

But I wasn't going to share all that with Rebel Tallard. "Because it's my name," I said stubbornly.

"My boy has a nickname too," Tallard said. "We call him Splinter." I didn't answer, but after a moment he went on like I had. "I'm a carpenter by trade. When my boy was just two or three years old, he began coming to the shop with me. He loved to watch me work, or play with the wood shavings and sawed-off bits. Someone once said he was a 'chip off the old block,' because he was so much like me. But someone else said, 'As young as that boy is, he's more like a splinter off the old block.' And the name stuck."

I wondered if he'd been dreaming of his son. "Is that Louis?" The question popped out.

Tallard jerked his head like I'd slapped him. His eyes went wide. I felt a sudden chill, like...like some haunt was looking out at me from his eyes.

Then he rubbed his hand over his face, and when he looked back at me, the ghost was gone. "Stephen. My son's real name is Stephen."

I considered asking Tallard about his nightmares, but for some reason didn't quite dare. Instead I asked, "How old is your boy?"

"Eleven. He was nine when I left home. I haven't seen him in two years."

His fingers scrabbled on the quilt for a moment, then closed around his tintype. With a shaking hand he brought it up so he could stare at it. I saw again those sad-eyed children and their mother, staring back.

I felt for that boy Splinter, spending two years without a pa. Almost against my will, I got up and heaved Tallard's feet back on the bed so he wasn't all twisted.

But I hated that boy Splinter, too. He lived in the South. He was a Rebel. His pa belonged to the army that killed my pa and brothers and my ma's fiddle-playing soul. I hated

Splinter and I hated his pa. Without another word I marched into the kitchen.

"Ma, if I get your fiddle, will you play?" I asked. She lifted her head and stared. "A Yankee song, Ma. Something fierce. 'The Battle Cry of Freedom,' or something."

Slowly she turned away, her eyes gone blank again. I sighed. Ma wasn't going to torment Tallard for me. I'd have to wait for the Yankees.

CHAPTER NINE

JULY 8–9, 1863

We heard the guns when the cavalry scrapped again on the afternoon of July 8. First, the Rebels pushed the Yankees away toward Boonsboro. Then, the Yankees shoved back, until the Rebels were crunched up toward Hagerstown and Williamsport. And in the middle of it all, one of the fiercest thunderstorms in memory lashed across the valley. I heard later the cavalrymen couldn't manage their horses in the deep mud, and had to fight dismounted, peering through the rain to make sure they were firing at the right people.

Those Rebels were no quitters. I'll give them that. They had their backs against the river and the whole Yankee army still hovering somewhere—*somewhere*—nearby. But those stubborn devils made it clear that they weren't giving in. They buzzed up and down the Potomac like bees at a hive. At Williamsport, the pitiful little shuttle they'd rigged to the Virginia bank was still slowly ferrying a few of the wounded at a time to safety.

The river was still too high to ford, but across from Falling Waters the Rebels were banging together a crazy-looking bridge. They'd scrounged up a few leaky old boats from somewhere, and the stench of boiling tar covered up the stink of rotting cow and fish. They built more with lumber stolen from Shoop and Lefever's lumberyard and torn-down buildings, and began hammering together a plank road to lay over the boats. They stole every scrap of lumber from the yard, and from Steffey's too.

On July 9 the rain stopped, giving us the first pleasant day we'd had in three weeks. Ma stood in the doorway sniffing like a coon dog, then turned her face to the sun. "I do crave a dry spell," she murmured.

I couldn't echo her wish. A dry spell meant the river waters would be coming down. And still the Yankees didn't show in force to liberate Williamsport. *Hurry, hurry…*All day I sent my silent message to the northeast, trying to will the Yankees to keep moving and finish their job. All day I listened, straining, aching to hear them come.

When I couldn't abide being at home a minute longer I walked into town and headed for Charley Troxell's blacksmith shop, where before the war men had always gathered to argue the merits of nightcrawlers and grubs for landing catfish, and hear whose prize mare had birthed a colt, and predict the weather. In those days talk had always been lively, and while Charley banged his anvil he kept the coffeepot near the coals for those who stopped by, and sometimes I ended up in the corner near a little picture of a naughty woman that Charley had nailed up in the corner.

But Charley had taken his tools—even his bellows, and anvil—and left town after a year or so of war. He got tired of having soldiers banging on his door all hours of the day and night, wanting him to shoe their horses, mend a broken axle, or re-tire the wheel on a supply wagon. And there were hardly any men left to spit tobacco juice and try to be heard above the hammer's clang.

A few still came, though. Habit, I guess. The day I stopped by Robert was watching Old Simp Hepplewhite play marbles with Abner Ainsminger. Abner had been discharged from the Union army with a bad case of pleurisy and rheumatism after two years of sleeping on the ground. He came home with ghosts in his eyes and a cough that seemed enough to pull out his very innards. He wasn't up to working yet, so I don't know what he and his widowed mother were living on—besides turnips from Agnes's garden, anyway.

I was still puzzling over the Yankees' strange case of The Slows. Why hadn't the Yankees come down while it was just the wagon train of wounded and their escort clogged up in town? "It seems to me they could've swung around and grabbed these here Rebels up," I said that afternoon.

"I thought the Yankee *would* swoop down, sure as you're born," Robert agreed, then looked at me anxiously to make sure we were still in agreement. Robert liked to be in agreement. "Sure as you're born. Don't know why they didn't. Could've had them."

"Ain't that simple." Abner squinted at his shooter carefully. "The Yanks won that fight at Gettysburg. But they're beat up bad too. Can't move a whole army overnight."

"But the Rebels got here. Why couldn't the Yankees?" I still didn't understand it.

"Plain to see you're not a general," Abner snorted, but I noticed he didn't really answer my question, either. Maybe he would have, but a spate of hacking seemed to steal most of his breath.

"Those Rebel boys are fixing for another fight," Hepplewhite reported. He had a high voice, which always made him sound excited. "They're digging in like gophers. And there's been fighting already, you know, all around. Yankee cavalry's a-feeling the Rebel lines, and the Rebel cavalry's a-pushin' 'em back. Ha!" He cackled in triumph as his marble knocked one of Abner's from the circle.

Abner scowled. "Those Rebels don't want to put up a fight unless they got to," he pointed out. "All they want to do right now is get across the river and lick their wounds."

"Yes," Robert agreed nervously. His head had been swinging back and forth so his good eye could keep up with whoever was talking.

"I don't think there's going to be a proper battle," I said stubbornly. "I think the Yankees are going to come and capture all the Rebs, and cart them off to prison camps."

Abner hooted like a saw-whet owl, which wasn't too smart, because it set him to coughing again. "You think those Rebs are just going to put up their hands and surrender, Chig?" he managed after a moment. "You think they're just going to pack themselves in train cars to get hauled off to one of your prison camps? They'll fight, all right."

"Maybe not." I sighed, looking around the dim, dusty shop, wishing like anything that Charley would walk in the door to light his fire and pump the bellows and bring a sense of life back into the room.

"If the choice is fight or go to a prison camp, they'll fight. Mark my words." Old Simp slumped on his belly, lining up his next shot. "I've heard tell of those camps. It's a slow death. They're hellholes."

"Not as bad as Southern prison camps," Abner protested. "Those Rebs, they starve our boys in prison camps. Just starve 'em. And shoot 'em too, sometimes, just for the fun of it. They pack 'em in without enough shelter or food or clothes. Our boys die off like rotten sheep in the camps."

"Maybe it's worse in the south," Old Simp allowed grudgingly. "But from the way I hear it, the Northern camps aren't a heap better."

"Yankee guards would be fair," I protested. "They're Yankees."

"I'll tell you what," Robert burst out, surprising us all. "I'll tell you what. Last spring I got hired on a farm in Frederick County to help get the crops in. I won't say which one." He looked both surprised and pleased to have information to share. "The family's trying to stay out of the war, mostly, but they have a nephew who went into the Rebel army, and got captured and sent to a Yankee prison camp. He died there, but not before getting some letters smuggled out somehow. They told of terrible things."

"It's a hard, slow death," Abner allowed. He sounded grim, maybe comparing it to his own health. I couldn't say. "No way for any man to end up. I'll wager any Rebel out there digging right now would rather take a bullet through the heart than get captured and shipped off."

I chewed that information over. Would Tallard rather get shot through the heart than captured? He didn't have any choice. Walking to our front door the other day had just about done him in. It wasn't too likely he'd find his way out to the fortifications his comrades were so busy digging, where he might get killed outright in a fight.

Well, it was of no matter to me. One way or another, the Yankees would finish him and his kind off...if they arrived before the Potomac River went down. *Hurry...hurry...*

CHAPTER TEN

JULY 10–11, 1863

On the tenth, a fight unrolled nearby at Funkstown. It wasn't close enough to be a real danger to us, although we heard the rumble of guns all day, and from the top of Cemetery Hill I could see puffs of smoke. I had high hopes, for a while, but it didn't come to much. After watching for a while I went home.

I was hauling in a bucket of drinking water when that Rebel Surgeon Hatfield arrived, come to check on Tallard. He still had that hollow-eyed, shaking-hand look to him. Now that I'd stuck my head in one of the hospitals, though, I didn't mark it down as hard drink any more. If I spent my days and nights trying to sort out the horrors of an army hospital, I'd probably have hollow eyes and shaking hands too.

"How are you making out, Captain?" Hatfield asked, bending over the bed.

"As well as can be expected."

"They treating you right?" Hatfield shot a look at the corner I'd squeezed myself into. I wanted to hear whatever was going to be said. Maybe there was some important information I could pass along to the Yankees. You never knew.

"They're treating me right," Tallard said quietly.

I wondered again why Tallard didn't tell on me for yanking that pillow away and leaving him to bleed to death. Had he been so feverish he didn't even realize? Just the thought brought back a little sick curl to my stomach, and I shoved that remembrance away.

Tallard had something else on his mind anyway. "Say doctor, can I show you my family?" A faint smile twitched around the corners of his mouth as he held up the tintype. "That's my wife, of course…and Splinter, he was nine when this was taken. Eliza, beside him, she was four."

"They're fine-looking children," Hatfield nodded, although he'd barely glanced at the image. "Now, let me change the bandage on your arm."

I couldn't pull my gaze away, but the surgeon leaned forward and blocked my vision before I could see what Tallard's stump looked like beneath the bloody, pus-stained strip of cloth bound over it. When Hatfield was finished he took a look at Tallard's second wound, where a ball had angled in between two ribs and exited two inches later, below his armpit.

"These are healing up as well as can be expected," Hatfield sighed. "Now listen, Captain. We've rigged up a ferry down at the ford, and we've started getting some of the wounded across. It's slow going. We can only take a few at a time. And we started with those who thought they were strong enough to walk to a town once we got them across—"

"I don't think I could walk very far." Tallard's voice was thin as parchment.

"Perhaps not. But now we've got a few Virginia farmers helping out on the other side. You need to rest up best as you can, and gather your strength, because someone will be coming to fetch you within the next day or so. Do you understand?"

Tallard nodded slowly.

"With any luck, we'll get you in line down by the ferryboats. But you need to know that General Lee's not planning on leaving anyone behind. He's got his best engineers working on a bridge. If we don't get all the wounded across by ferry, we'll wagon the rest over on the bridge. So hang on. Store up your strength. You'll be home in Virginia in no time."

I clenched my jaw. I didn't want to think about Tallard making it home. While the Yankees dawdled and stalled, Tallard was slowly getting stronger. Just that morning he'd made it to the outhouse and back, all on his own. Now the surgeon was laying out a plan to get him across the Potomac.

As if sensing my anger, the surgeon wiped his hands on his trousers and fixed me with a stern look. "Are you feeding this man well, boy?"

"He doesn't get much. But he gets as much as we have." That was the truth.

"I'll send more provisions around if I can," Hatfield said, then turned back to Tallard. "Don't forget what I said, Captain. You're going home."

That surgeon didn't know or care that *my* pa was never coming home, or my brothers either. I stormed out of the house and spent an hour pitching rocks out of the torn-up garden. Most made a good *thunk* against the stable wall.

"Hey Chigger, what're you doing?"

Robert was standing at the edge of the garden, a lumpy sack slung over his shoulder. For a long moment I was tempted to spill it all out to Robert: the hurt, the anger, the ache of missing my father and brothers, the worry for Ma. Then I remembered that Robert's own folks were long dead, and his mules stolen, and the shack he'd called home washed away.

"Just pitching rocks," I sighed. "What've you been doing?"

"Farmer Ballweg hired me on to help haul his wheat sheaves in." Robert sounded glum. He'd rather drive mules for miles on the canal towpath than do field work. "Those sheaves were mucky-wet. But the Rebs keep stealing 'em, for feed and bedding and such. And some cavalry rode right through, and churned some of it under. So he figured he'd haul in what he could, and see if he could save some of it."

He shook his head. "I don't know why those Rebs couldn't have just gone around. I just don't know."

"I don't know either."

Robert swung the sack around and dumped it on the ground. "Old Ballweg said he couldn't pay me until he sells some of his wheat. If he does. But he did give me these. I brought 'em for you and your mother."

I stared at several cucumbers, some carrots, two fists of new string beans, some radishes...even a ham bone. My mouth began to water. Finally, I jerked my gaze away. "Robert, you don't have to share these with us," I managed.

He looked as confused as if I'd told him he didn't have to breathe. "But you're lettin' me sleep in your stable."

I didn't argue further. That evening I ate the best meal I could remember. Robert wouldn't come inside and eat with us—he was scared of Tallard—but I took his bowl out to him, and kept him company while he ate. "Umm, this sure is good," he said happily, scraping the bowl with his spoon. "Chigger, be sure to thank your ma for me, will you?"

I nodded, feeling somehow more settled than I had in a while. "Sure, Robert. I'll tell her."

Father Ryan finally showed up the next day to check on Ma. It was another hot, damp day, and I noticed how shabby his robe looked. I left them alone in the kitchen for a while, but when it seemed like a goodly amount of time had passed, I headed back inside to make sure I didn't miss saying good-bye to the priest. When I went in the front door, there was no sign of Ma, but Father Ryan was crouching by Tallard's bed.

Without a word I turned and walked back out.

Father Ryan found me a few minutes later, sitting under one of the cherry trees. I crossed my arms. Father plunked right down in the mud beside me. "You're angry because I was speaking with the wounded Confederate."

"No I'm not," I said, but the words sounded angry even to my own ears.

"When I asked if I could do something for him, he asked me to pray for his family. That's not a request worth anger, lad."

"What about my family?" I demanded.

Father Ryan put a hand on my shoulder. "Your family is in my prayers every day, Chigger. Every day."

Maybe it was the weight of his hand, or maybe it was the kindness in his voice, but my anger melted like ice in July. "I'm sorry, Father," I mumbled, staring at the ground. "I never seem to know what to…what's what, anymore." He waited, and I told him what had happened the day before. "I was so angry…then Robert shared his food with us. Robert doesn't have anything but the clothes on his back, and he shared his food…" My words trailed away. I picked at a clot of mud on my ankle.

Father Ryan nodded. "Sometimes the simplest act of kindness can mean the most. Robert's kindness fed your body *and* your soul."

I didn't want to talk about souls, not when I'd tried to commit murder in the last week, and spent a lot of time wishing a man dead, or at least captured and sent to prison camp. "What's the news from town?" I asked. "I haven't been in yet today."

He sighed. "I've no news worth the telling. A few more wounded men died in the night. As for the armies…the Yankee army is pushing ever closer. I heard an officer say that the Yankee cavalry keeps trying to find a weak spot in the Confederate line. But no one seems to know why they haven't launched a full assault. It's all a wretched business."

I shook my head. A week had gone by, almost, and I was starting to believe I'd never see a Yankee-blue uniform again. "Well, I thank you for visiting Ma," I said. "She sets a store by you. How did you find her?"

He seemed to choose his words carefully. "She is struggling, I know."

"I worry, Father. I worry that…that she'll go away from me. Sometimes she stops talking, just sits and stares at the wall."

"She is still living with terrible grief. We have to help her find reasons to keep going."

I picked up a twig and twiddled it in my fingers. "She's afraid I'm going to go off to war too."

"You're too young—"

"I don't know that my father would be saying the same thing, if he was here," I pointed out. "The Irish are fighters. Folks say the Irish Brigade is one of the best in the whole Yankee army! Even the Protestants say that. We don't run from a good fight. And Patrick went off to avenge Pa and Egan, and I think Liam went off to avenge Patrick—"

"Chigger," Father Ryan said sternly, "vengeance is not a good reason for a boy to even think of going to war."

"It's not so much me thinking," I defended myself. "I'm just trying to figure out who to honor. How can I choose, if my mother's wishes don't match my father's?"

"Your mother is living, lad."

Yes, I thought. But you don't see those O'Malley eyes staring from the mantelpiece every day. You don't hear the unspoken messages when I visit the graves on Cemetery Hill. And you're not telling me how to take care of Ma, and keep her from sinking inside. You're not telling me how to keep her fed through the coming winter, when there's nothing left of the place and no one looking to hire a runty boy like me.

"Oh Chigger," Father Ryan sighed. "You must have faith. You'll find your path. That's all I can promise."

I had no reason to feel sure about that. I shoved to my feet. "Thank you again for coming out, Father."

As I watched the tired, dirty young priest walk back down our lane, I realized his words had helped me, even if I wasn't sure quite how. I still felt lost. But it was nice to know that Father Ryan, like Robert, cared enough to do a kind turn for the O'Malleys. Somehow, that did give me a shred of hope.

CHAPTER ELEVEN

JULY 12, 1863

That Sunday morning was the first Sunday I could remember that we didn't wash up and go to mass. But with the town full of Rebels, and the churches all turned into hospitals, there was nowhere to go. It seemed odd to have a Sunday come like just another day, but there it was.

After breakfast I was of a mind to tackle some chores. It was, I'll wager, the hottest morning of the year. The rain held off, but I was still wringing wet by the time I'd walked to the woodpile.

Wood was scarce because the soldiers took whatever they could find. But I'd been scrambling in the woods for deadfall and such, and kept a little pile behind the falling-in stable. We didn't go through a lot, this time of year. But I needed to keep Ma supplied with stovewood for cooking. I went at it for half an hour or so before I heard someone call my name.

"Chigger."

Tallard stood in the yard. His hand was pressed against the bullet hole in his side, but he was less hunched over than I'd seen him yet. He's getting stronger, I thought, and

wondered for the thousandth time, *Where are the Yankees?*
"What?"

"Your mother needs tending."

Quick as summer lightning I shoved the axe up on a
handy log—out of sight, I hoped, from any thieving Rebels
that might chance to pass through. Then I ran past Tallard.

Ma's wails tore out of the house. I found her in a heap
on the floor of the main room, pooled in that black mourning
dress she wore.

I dropped on my knees beside her. "Ma, what is it?"

"My boys," she sobbed. "My boys."

She was clutching the tintypes of Pa and my brothers
in her lap. Seeing them brought the usual stab to my own
heart too. Those blurry scraps of tin were all we had left of
the noisy men who had posed with such gallantry. As I gently pulled them from her, I noticed the tiny calluses on the
tips of those fingers that had once danced across the fiddle
strings. It took everything I had not to start bawling too. I laid
the tintypes aside with shaking hands, then tugged Ma to
her feet. "Come on into the kitchen. Please, Ma. I'll get you a
cup of water, and find you a handkerchief."

She let me lead her like a halter-broke calf into the
kitchen, and her sobs faded to heaving snuffles. "Oh Chig,"
she managed finally. "Sometimes it's too hard to bear. Promise me you won't go off and get yourself killed too."

I ladled up some water, stumbling about for words. For
some reason the usual reassurances didn't come. "I don't
want to go," I said finally. "But Ma, sometimes I feel like Pa
and the boys would want me to. They'd want me to stand up
for what they believed was right. Fight for their sake."

"But I don't want you to go!" Her voice was shrill, and
the light in her eyes so frantic that I eased off.

"Don't cry again. I'm not making any plans to go." That
much was the truth. It was impossible to make plans when I
didn't know what was right or wrong. So much easier to live
from day to day, and put off making any choices.

After I got Ma settled I went back into the main room. Tallard had waited outside 'til after I got Ma on her feet, but I found him flopped back across the bed. "Is she well?"

"No thanks to you." I fixed him with a glare. "Did you say something to her?"

"I didn't…" He swallowed whatever he was going to say with a sigh.

I picked up the photographs I'd left on the floor and started to arrange them back on the mantelpiece. Tallard may not have said or done something to set her off this time. But he and his kind had brought this misery down on our house. I stared for a moment at the images already scratched into my brain as if with a branding iron. Had Tallard fought in any of the battles they had? Surely so—

"What were they like?" he asked softly.

The simple question rooted me to the spot like a club-stunned hog. *Alive*, I wanted to say. Not quiet and scrawny like me, but so full of life it had exploded from them.

For a moment I was all set to turn away, not wanting to tarnish their memory by trotting it out before this Rebel. But something kept me from it. Maybe I wanted Tallard to know, to understand, what he'd done.

Slowly I held one tintype before his eyes. "This was my Pa. He was…" I had to stop.

Tallard's gaze was steady. "What was he like?" he asked again.

So I tried to tell him. I told how Pa had brought Ma and Egan and baby Patrick from the Great Hunger in Ireland. How they'd spent a year in the miserable tenements of New York City before Pa found work in Maryland as a laborer along the C & O Canal. I told how he was quick to anger but quicker to laugh. I told how he made sure that each of his boys knew how to fish. I told how his stories of his boyhood in Ireland kept listeners begging for more.

Once I started talking it was hard to stop. The words came like floodwaters pushing at the riverbanks. So, next I told Tallard how, like Pa, Egan was loud and laughing and never one to shy from a fight. And a favorite with the girls, sure enough. Egan always had pretty girls waiting in line to dance with him. "I think Egan thought the war would be a lark. He was full of steam about proving what Irish Catholics could do to earn their keep, and defending the country that gave us asylum from the British. And Pa laughed and said the Irish never shied from a fight, and that he might as well go along and keep Egan out of trouble."

"What happened to them?"

"They joined up with some of Pa's old friends, in the 69th New York Regiment, that became the heart of the Irish Brigade. They fought at Bull Run. It was their first battle—"

"Mine too," Tallard said, and for a moment those ghosts were back in his eyes.

"And they got shot." I swallowed hard. "They both died in hospitals. Egan went first, but Pa wasn't long after."

I realized I'd somehow come to be perching on the edge of Tallard's bed. I didn't like being so familiar with him, but at the same time, something inside was fiercely glad to be making Tallard understand that the Yankees he and his kind killed weren't just names and numbers. They were fathers and sons and brothers. I hoped it would give him something to think about when he was sitting in a prison camp.

The next likeness I held up was Patrick's. "Patrick went into a rage when Pa and Egan got killed." It had been a cold, thundering anger. Ma had sobbed and Patrick had thrown things and I hadn't known what to say to calm either one down. "He enlisted pretty quick. He wanted to avenge Pa and Egan, he said. He got shot through the gut at the battle of Antietam Creek last September. Just a few miles away at Sharpsburg. Liam went down and fetched his body home."

I pulled out Liam's photograph, remembering the haunted look in Liam's eyes when he returned from the battle-field at Antietam Creek in a rented wagon, with the lonely coffin in back. "Liam had just turned seventeen. He never was as talkative as the others, and he didn't say much about losing Patrick. He just up and married his girl Agnes, and marched off. He fathered a child and didn't live to see it born. He was dead by spring. He got killed at a place called Chancellorsville." I swiped at a hot tear. "His captain wrote and said he'd taken a ball clean through the heart. But later we got a letter from one of his pards who said he'd seen a cannonball blow Liam to pieces. No one ever did find a body to send home, so I figure the second story was the true one."

For a moment I stared at Liam's serious face. He was wearing his uniform, standing in front of a painted canvas in some photographer's tent, rifle at his side. Grief was a dull knife twisting my innards. What was it about Liam's death that hurt so particular? Was it because he'd been closest to me in age? Was it not having a body to bury? Was it in knowing that he was dead before Willis was even born?

Tallard's low voice pulled me from my thoughts. "Chigger...for whatever it's worth, I'm sorry for your losses."

I folded my arms tight across my chest. "That's not worth anything." Words couldn't undo what bullets and cannonballs had done.

As usual, my anger didn't anger Tallard. I wished it would. I would have lit into him without regret if he had. Instead, all he said was, "You and your mother have known unbearable sorrow." He was still staring at the wall.

I suddenly realized I didn't want this Rebel thinking my ma—my real ma—was the woman he'd seen sobbing on the floor. I glanced at the kitchen door, then dropped my voice. "My mother wasn't like this before the war." I pointed to the fiddle hanging on the wall. "That belongs to her. She brought it from Ireland. She's the best fiddler in the county. She'd play, and folks would laugh and sing and dance—" I stopped sudden as a balky mule. Those memories were too dear to share with a Rebel after all.

"I've seen women like her," Tallard murmured sadly. "Too many women. Some find a way to keep going. Some don't."

Something cold skittered through my chest. Tallard was echoing my own fear. I covered up by lashing out. "It's all the

Rebels' fault. You and your cursed army, fighting against your own country."

I bit off the flow of words, waiting for him to tell me that plenty of Southern women were suffering too. He pressed his lips together for a moment, but all he finally said was, "Didn't you say your brother Liam fathered a child before he left?"

"Yes. Willis. He was born a few weeks ago."

"Where is he?"

"He lives with his mother Agnes, and Agnes's parents."

"Far away?"

I frowned, wondering why he was asking. "No, the other side of Williamsport. Why do you care?"

"I was just wondering. It seems like a baby might go a long way toward keeping your mother going. Keeping her from giving up."

I considered that. "The two families don't mix much. Agnes isn't Catholic. She's real nice, though. I keep an eye on her, now Liam's gone. She's invited Ma to come and visit Willis. And I've suggested it to Ma. But Ma won't go."

"Don't ask your mother," Tallard said gently. "Don't suggest. Just go fetch Agnes and Willis and bring them here for a visit."

I hesitated, a storm of conflict. Part of me thought it was a good idea. Part of me was ashamed I hadn't thought of it myself. Part of me wished that *I* was enough to keep Ma's heart alive. Part of me was angry that I was even having this conversation with a cursed Rebel.

Tallard shifted in bed and a grimace of pain crossed his face. "It might work," he managed. "I remember my own mother, after my father died. Nothing seemed to interest her until one of my sisters put a grandbabe in her arms."

I got up and carefully lined the tintypes back on the mantel, and draped the strips of black crepe over each just the way Ma liked them, all the while letting my thoughts tumble like coal from a canalboat at the warehouse. Might

Tallard have a good idea? Was I a fool to even think of taking advice from a Rebel?

Chigger O'Malley, make a decision, I finally ordered myself.

And just as quick, I ducked my head into the kitchen. "Ma, you all right here for a bit? I'm going for a walk."

Agnes looked startled by my request. "Oh Chig, I don't know. I'm happy to let Willis spend time with your mother. But this isn't a good time."

I'd found her in the yard, taking advantage of the dry afternoon to peg out sheets across the line. From Agnes's shoved-up sleeves, the tired lines in her face, the rings of sweat staining her brown dress, I guessed they'd been boiled and scrubbed like nobody's business. But she hadn't been able to scrub away all of the bloodstains. I wondered if we were all cursed to fight with bloodstains, in our linens and in our hearts, for the rest of our lives.

Willis gurgled from a basket nearby, in the wall's shade, where he was wrapped in a sheet. I dug a toe into the crusted mud, considering. Now that I was here, I wasn't eager to give up so easily. "I know it's a hard time. But my ma is doing poorly, Agnes. Real poorly. I'm scared for her. I'm afraid she's going to give up. She needs...she needs a reason to keep getting out of bed every day."

"Here, help me with this." Agnes handed me one corner of a wet sheet, and we struggled to stretch it over the line without dragging it in the mud. "I'm sorry, Chig. Real sorry. But I don't dare leave home right now. I've still got a house full of Rebels, and no word from mother and father. We can't come right now."

I looked at Willis, remembering the feel of him in my arms. Liam's child. "Would you let me take him?"

Agnes whipped her head around. "No! Willis doesn't go anywhere without me."

"I wouldn't keep him long, Agnes. I promise. And I'd be careful. Ever so careful."

"Chig, there are soldiers all over town! And the Yankees could get here any minute. All the Rebels here are jumpy as hares. They get edgier every day. I know they're just waiting for the attack. It could come any minute. What if the Yankees start shelling, and a cannonball lands on you?"

"A cannonball could land on the house here just as easy," I pointed out. "Please, Agnes."

She faced me with a desperate look in her eyes. "Chig, can't you understand, Willis is my boy! He's all I've got left of Liam. He's my son. If anything happened to him, I'd..."

Her voice trailed off. Those anguished eyes bored into mine. I wondered if she was suddenly imagining herself in my mother's place, with three sons and a husband dead and gone.

The back door banged open and a Rebel stuck his head out. "Mrs. O'Malley! The surgeon's asking for you. He needs help with that boy in the front bedroom."

"Coming," Agnes called, without turning her head.

I didn't realize until she'd gathered up Willis and laid him in my arms that I'd been holding my breath.

"Chigger O'Malley, you tend this baby with your life. You hear me?"

I nodded. "I swear, Agnes. First sign of trouble, I'll duck into somebody's house. And once I get him home, you know my ma will tend him good. She knows all about babies."

Agnes was fussing with the sheet. "Keep him out of the sun. It's hot enough to fry the devil."

"I will."

"I fed him just before you came, so he should be good. Have him back within two hours, though. I mean it."

"I promise," I said, then headed out of there before she could change her mind.

I hurried back through town, fast as I could. Willis started fretting before we'd crossed Potomac Street, and was letting loose with good hearty wails by the time I reached Church Street. That tiny babe was awkward as a sack of potatoes in my arms. All the soldiers on the street turned their heads as

I shoved past. Several laughed, and one older man—an officer, by the looks of him—hollered, "For God's sake, boy, get that baby off the street!" And I heard one say sadly, "Oh, my little one did that the morning I left. I wonder what she sounds like now."

I didn't have the faintest notion what to do for Willis and began to wonder if I'd made a mighty mistake after all. When I happened past Widow Ainsminger it took all my resolve not to shove him into her arms.

"Why Chigger O'Malley, where are you going with that baby?" she asked in surprise. She was carrying a big basket of bandages and such on her hip, but stopped square in my path.

"I'm taking Willis to my mother."

She stepped from the path, nodding, and I hurried on my way.

By the time I turned in our own yard on the south side of town Willis had stopped wailing, although he was still snuffling a bit, sounding sorely annoyed. When I pushed in our front door, the sound pulled Ma from the kitchen.

"What?..." she asked, her eyes going wide with surprise. She stopped stone-still, arms at her sides.

"It's Willis, Ma. Agnes let me borrow him for a visit." I hesitated, trying to hold out the baby without losing my grip on him. I'd hoped Ma would scoop him right up, but she still didn't move. Helpless, I glanced at Tallard. The Reb jerked his head toward Ma.

I moved toward her. "Take him," I ordered, and her arms came up. Once she had Willis I tugged her to the rocking chair in the corner.

Somehow, even though she still looked dazed, Ma knew how to get Willis settled down again, and back to sleep. I left them to it, and went back outside to finish chopping some firewood. But when I figured our two hours were almost up, and went back inside, I thought I heard the faint hum of a lullaby. And when I eased Willis away her arms lingered in the air, reluctant to let go.

I wrapped Willis back in his sheet before heading back. I was already out the door before Ma finally found something to say. "Tell Agnes I wouldn't mind tending Willis again," she called.

"I'll tell her," I echoed. I was pleased with that, but something felt odd. I'd gone well into town before I realized what it was. I was smiling.

CHAPTER TWELVE

JULY 12, 1863

Agnes was waiting tearfully at the front door. She snatched Willis from my arms and covered his little bald head with kisses. "Oh Chigger, thank God," she managed finally. "I've been watching and watching for you."

"He's fine," I said, feeling a mite defensive.

"I've been so worried." Agnes gave me a watery smile. "I heard the surgeon inside talking to one of the other officers. The officer said the Yankees are close enough to spit on. He said he'd heard that General Lee is terribly anxious, waiting for all hell to break loose." A sudden flush stained her thin white cheeks. "Excuse my language, that was a quote. They can't figure out why it hasn't happened already. It was so frightening to think of a battle starting and Willis being—being out there, somewhere." She lay her cheek on Willis's head. "Oh, and you too, of course."

I was used to being an afterthought. "I'm sorry it was so hard on you," I told her. "And I do thank you. Willis is fine, really. I just think maybe he needs a clean linen." I couldn't help sniffing the arm of my shirt where I'd been holding him.

"I'll see to it. But Chig?" She put a hand on my shoulder as I started to turn back down the steps. "Did it help your mother to see him?"

I grinned, in spite of everything. "It surely did, Agnes. It surely did. I'm more beholden to you than I can say."

Agnes nodded. "Mothers set a tremendous store in their boys. I do understand. Tell your mother that I'll bring Willis out again as soon as I think it's safe. Or…or you bring her in here. In fact…" She chewed her lip for a moment, then seemed to decide something. "In fact, you and your mother are welcome to come and stay here for a while, if you'd like. It's hard on me to tend all these Rebels and mind Willis at the same time. And even after my parents get back…I'm sure they wouldn't mind. We've got plenty of room. These are hard times. Willis needs all the family he's got left."

I was struck dumb. The last thing I ever expected was for Agnes to suggest such a thing. How would Ma take to it? Would she be willing to leave our own place? The home she'd made with my pa, the bed where she'd birthed all her boys? It seemed unlikely…then I recalled the look in her eyes when I took Willis back from her, the tone in her voice when she called after me. Maybe it wasn't so unlikely at that.

"Thank you, Agnes," I told her, right from my heart. "I'll talk to her. I believe she'll come."

I was so full of thoughts about the idea of me and Ma moving into the big frame house near Conococheague Creek that as I started back through town I didn't notice, at first, what was different. Then it started to seep into my brain, like water pushing through hard-packed soil. Williamsport's streets were as clogged with Rebels, and their mules and ambulances and supply wagons and artillery and such, as they'd been for a week. It was still hard to walk without getting jostled and hard to hear a single voice among the din of shouts. But the commotion suddenly seemed somehow more frantic.

I was trying to figure that out when my ears happened to pick out a wagon driver bellowing at his skeletal mules as they tried to inch forward among the crowd. "Come on there, you dang cusses. You cain't go dropping dead on me 'til we get to Virginny, you hear? We're headed for the river, you cantankerous mules, and I aim on gettin' across this after-noon if it's the last thing I do."

Gettin' across this afternoon...

The Rebels had started to cross the Potomac.

It took me a long time to shove and elbow and squeeze my way toward the warehouse basin and the ford. The whole area was so jammed with Rebel wagons that I finally gave up and headed up Cemetery Hill. It was crowded with Rebels and a few townsfolk who'd piled up to the high ground for a look-see, but being puny, I managed to pinch through. When I finally had a good view, I stared down to the ford below. My jaw and my heart dropped at the same time.

A line of wagons was in the water just downstream of the ferry cable, pulled by horses and mules bobbing in the Potomac's fast current. From the hill's height they were tiny as toys but I could almost feel them struggling, fighting, des-perate to make the Virginia shore. It wasn't an easy cross-ing. But they were crossing.

"I got to hand it to ole Marse Robert," a Rebel standing near me said. He bit off the end of a cigar and spat it on the ground. "I got to say, a week ago I didn't figure to see this sight."

"General Lee don't give up easy," his friend allowed. "But don't sing 'Dixie' yet. We got 4,000 wagons to get across. And the river still looks purty high to me. I don't know when they'll start marching us troops across, but I don't aim to scoot away from the Yanks just to drown crossing the Potomac."

"I heard the river's fallen 18 inches in the last 24 hours," the first man said. "If that keeps up, we may be able to ford on foot by tomorrow morning."

"That's if it don't rain again." The other soldier sniffed the air. "And it sure smells like rain to me."

I edged away so I didn't have to hear their bickering. I didn't care about the details. All I knew was the Rebels had started their escape across the river. And where the bloody blazes were the Yankees? Why didn't they come? I was so angry I could hardly see straight. The Rebels and the Yankees had fought on the same field at Gettysburg. The Rebels had had time to retreat south to Williamsport and sit for a week, running their little ferry and building a new bridge. And still the Yankees hadn't shoved down after them to snatch them all up? I couldn't understand it. Plum couldn't understand it.

I hated the sight but I couldn't leave. Even when a short, hard thunderstorm blew through, I couldn't bring myself to go home. Maybe the Potomac will rise again, I thought hopefully, but the Rebels below kept feeding their wagons into the river, one by one. Evening came and my stomach was growling with hunger and the folks around me came and went. The Rebels managed to light bonfires on the shore below, and I spotted several more on the Virginia shore, to guide the wagoners over.

Before finally heading home I slipped over to the knoll where my pa and brothers were buried—everyone but Liam, anyway, and I'd hammered a wooden cross into the ground for him just the same. The area was away from the viewing edge of the hill, for which I was truly thankful. If I'd found a couple of filthy Rebels lounging on my family graves I don't know what would have happened.

I knelt in the mud, soaked and shivering a bit now that the day's fierce heat was behind. "Pa," I whispered, "I'm ever so sorry, but the Rebels are starting to get away. I don't know what's happened to the Yankees, Pa. I just don't."

A burst of laughter punched through the evening behind me. I hesitated, and looked over my shoulder to make sure no one was listening. The missing of my father was like a wave so powerful at that moment I felt near to drowning myself.

"I just don't know what to make of it all, Pa. I've been waiting and waiting for the Yankees to come and end the war. First, I wanted them to kill all the Rebels. Lately, I've been thinking how it might be good just to have all the Rebels taken prisoner and carted off to prison camps. But there's this one at our house, Tallard's his name...and he helped me with Ma, you see. He saved her when she lit into two Reb soldiers who came to steal our last cookpot. And he told me to go fetch Willis, and I think it worked. Ma wants to see Willis again, and Agnes said we could come and live with them. Just for a while," I added quickly. "I'll get the home place going again when I can.

"But anyway, this Tallard...I don't know what to make of him. Like I said, he helped me with Ma. I think...I really think I would have lost her if he hadn't been around. But he and his army killed you, and Egan, and Patrick, and Liam..." I fumbled into silence. I couldn't bring myself even to whisper that I'd lately had trouble wishing Tallard into prison and the long, slow death Robert and Abner had talked of. But every time that thought of mercy bubbled to the top of my mind, the image of all the dead O'Malley men marched through, and the flame of hatred sputtered back to life again.

"I'll try to do you all proud," I whispered helplessly to the silent graves, then headed down. The weight of their unspoken expectations was heavy on my shoulders.

Finally, halfway home, I decided to just give up wishing and hoping for this or that. The war was surely too big for anyone to make sense of, much less a boy so puny his own kin called him Chigger. Come what may, Tallard was on his own. It was up to the armies—the Rebels, and the Yankees—to decide Tallard's fate.

CHAPTER THIRTEEN

JULY 13, 1863

I didn't tell Tallard what I'd seen. His questioning gaze followed me like a puppy as I hauled kindling inside, and later brought him supper. I was glad to disappear into the kitchen, and try to hide in sleep. But Tallard had another bad night. He moaned in his sleep about that Louis fellow, and gave orders to "Keep your head down," and "Advance, double-quick," and once or twice cried out like he was getting bullet-hit all over again. I didn't get more than a scrap of rest.

Ma didn't ask about the soldiers but the next morning she did mention Willis. "I wouldn't mind seeing Liam's boy again, Chig," she said slowly, when she was cleaning up from our breakfast biscuits.

I hadn't yet told her about Agnes's offer. I needed time to sort everything out. "I know, Ma, and Agnes said she'd be glad of it too," I said instead, avoiding her eyes. "But...but the truth is, the Rebels are on the move. I don't want to have you or Willis out and about unless I'm sure it's safe."

I spent the morning hoeing our garden plot. Now mind, stragglers from both armies had cleared everything out. I had no crops coming and no seed to plant. But I didn't want to leave Ma that morning, and I had to have something to do. So I spent several hours breaking clods of wet earth and stamping out the ruts. Robert showed up mid-morning and helped for a spell, which was a lot.

That chore only lasted 'til noon or so, when Ma called me into the house for biscuits and tea. "I thank you," I told Robert. "Come in and eat?"

"No, Chigger. No." Robert looked worried. "Not with that Rebel in the house. Oh, no."

So I didn't even get Robert inside to help keep the conversation going that noon. By the time we'd eaten my good intentions were gone. I knew I was going to go plum crazy if I didn't get away from there. "I'm going out to see what's what," I announced. And I escaped from the log walls and the eyes of my dead father and brothers staring from the mantel, Ma's silence, and Tallard's watching eyes.

I walked into a misty gray afternoon threatening to give way into steady rain. Instead of circling first through Williamsport, I roamed toward the Rebel defensive lines. Sentries weren't letting folks go too far but I did worm my way out past town, where the farmers had tried so hard to wrestle a crop from their soaked and war-torn fields.

I'd grown so weary of waiting for the guns I hardly gave them mind, now. And I'd gotten so used to winding through the Rebels I hardly paid them mind either, just swam through them like an eel heading upstream. But I just about jumped out of my skin when the sudden ragged chords of a Yankee anthem, "The Battle Cry of Freedom," drifted through the mist:

Yes we'll rally 'round the flag, boys, rally once again
Shouting the battle cry of freedom
We will rally from the hillside, we'll gather from the plain
Shouting the battle cry of freedom!

The Union forever, hurrah, boys, hurrah
Down with the traitor, and up with the star
For we'll rally 'round the flag, boys, rally once again
Shouting the battle cry of freedom!

"What's that?" I asked a Rebel boy sitting by the road, picking at a crusted gash on his heel. He didn't look much older than me, and was filthy as a hog.

His look wondered if I was an idiot. "The Yanks."

"They're that close?" Why the devil were they singing, instead of charging forward?

"Yep." The boy shoved up and took a couple hobbling steps. "Lordy, I'd sell my soul for a pair of shoes. Anyway, they've been serenading us all morning."

I felt dumb as a fence post. I'd known war as a thing of terrible battles that killed O'Malley men, and a thing of sudden skirmishes that sent me and Ma tumbling to the root cellar. This part of war, this odd retreat from Gettysburg, was beyond all ken.

The mist cloaked most of the view from the top of Cemetery Hill. Still, it was clear that the Rebels had been at it all night. The little ferryboat was still slowly inching back and forth, carrying wounded soldiers to Virginia's safety. There were strings of wagons still jamming the road heading toward the ford, but there were lots less of them than there had been the day before. And unless I was mistaken, clogging the roads behind them were packs of Rebel infantry. Foot soldiers. I squinted at the trees near the Potomac's edge. I could tell by the muddy high-water marks on the trees that the flood had fallen off considerable. That Rebel General Lee, it seemed clear, planned on sending a good chunk of his infantry across as soon as the wagons were over.

If the drizzle and mist made it hard for me to see from so close, I knew any Yankee observers watching from some distant hill probably wouldn't realize the Rebels were planning a full-scale retreat across the Potomac that night. I wished like anything I could run down the hill and across the fields, just keep running until I could find some Yankee general. "You got to attack *now*!" I'd yell. "It looks like they're going to try to cross tonight!" But the Rebels' defensive line trapped me like a penned hog.

I watched for a while with an ache in my throat. Toward the Rebels' line of fortifications I made out a ring of flickering campfires. They were barely visible…and at the same time, it seemed like there were a lot of them. Finally I realized it was all part of the plan. The Rebels were holding lines of men in their trenches, and lighting lots of fires, to help fool the Yankees.

When I couldn't bear watching any longer I managed to claw through the throng to Agnes's house, to make sure she and Willis were still faring well. "They cleared me out an hour ago," she told me. "An ambulance came and they loaded all the wounded up and headed for the ford. I heard 'em say they'd gotten all the wounded out of Williamsport."

That meant they'd be collecting those they'd scattered among the homes and farms outside of town. Like Tallard. I heard again the eerie echo of Yankee voices through the mist. Close, so close… Would Tallard escape in time?

It's no concern of yours, I reminded myself, good and sharp. Still, I decided it was time to head for home.

There was a lot of traffic on our road south of town too. More columns of men, more cursing teamsters and creaking wagons, more couriers and officers trying to thread through on horseback. I figured the Rebel engineers must have finished the bridge at Falling Waters. Lee was splitting his army. Some to the Williamsport ford to cross on foot, some down to the bridge.

I found Ma standing at the end of our lane, watching the smelly Rebel tide flow south. I didn't like the look in her eyes. "Ma, come in before you're soaked through."

"Did you stop to see Agnes and the babe?"

"Yes. They're well, though Agnes looked fearsome tired. We'll go up there, Ma, when all of this is over. Agnes said we could come stay, if we wanted. She wants Willis to know you."

Ma nodded, but her eyes never left the soldiers straggling past. "Those men killed my boys," she said.

I swallowed hard and took her arm. "Come inside, Ma. There's nothing we can do about it now. Come inside."

Once in the house, Ma disappeared into the kitchen. Tallard's gaze stabbed at me, pulling me over like a gigged frog. "What's happening?" he asked quietly.

There was nothing to do but answer. "There's plenty of Rebels still standing guard in the fortifications. They're still building up forces there. But at the same time, it looks like the rest are trying to line up to get across the ford. Or head down toward Falling Waters. They've been working on a new bridge to Falling Waters."

"The river's down?"

I nodded slowly. "It was down enough last night that the Rebel wagoners started swimming their rigs over. It's still drizzly out. But…but I think the infantry is going to commence crossing tonight."

Tallard reached for the tintype of his family, propped on the log wall by his bed where a bit of rough chinking stuck out.

"They're rounding up the last of the wounded," I added. "They've cleared out all the buildings in town. Now they'll be heading out for the stragglers."

"Yes," Tallard said. "But the Yankees must be getting close."

I nodded. "The Yankee lines have pressed so close I could hear 'em singing. I don't know that your army's going to make it across before the Yankees attack. Nobody can figure out why they haven't attacked already."

He was staring at his children. I could guess what he was thinking. What he was wondering. The silence plucked on my nerves like nervous fingers on an ill-tuned fiddle. I wanted to get away from him but didn't know where to go. "Tell me about them," I finally heard myself say.

He blinked. "What?"

"Tell me about your family."

I thought for a moment he wasn't going to answer. Then, "My wife has been my true companion since I was six years old," he said slowly. "And the children…they're my greatest joy. I treasured them when I was with them…but I've come to know I didn't treasure them enough. Splinter, he's quick and bright. And good with his hands. I always imagined we'd one day have a shop together. 'Tallard and Son.' I've imagined the sign a thousand times."

I heard the sudden memory of my own Pa's voice, ringing through the years. "Maybe one day we'll take over the cement mill," he boomed, the day he'd been first hired to labor there. "I can see it, can't you?" And when Ma had smiled at his exuberance, he waved her doubts aside like a pesky fly. "I can see it now. 'O'Malley and Sons...'"

I'd been a wee boy, and had almost forgotten Pa's dream. Something like bile rose in my throat.

But Tallard didn't notice, and his voice nailed me in place. "And Eliza, she was full of mischief. She tried her mama's patience sorely. And I'm afraid I didn't help by laughing when I came home and heard the tales—"

"Why?"

The question startled him. "Why what?"

I wanted to pound the infernal Rebel. "Why did the South start this evil war? Why did you leave your family and march off? Why? *Why?*" I heard my voice rising like a child about to bawl, and finally choked off the stream of questions.

"The South didn't start this war," Tallard said slowly, staring at the ceiling. "As for the rest...why I left...I knew the answer, once. I can't seem to find it any more. You want simple answers. There aren't any."

That wasn't good enough, but I couldn't find words to trap my rage and grief. I took a deep breath and bundled them away. And when the silence got uncomfortable I asked a simpler question instead. "What is it like to be in a battle?" I wanted to know. I wanted to understand what my father and brothers had understood.

"They're all different," Tallard said slowly. He laid his tintype facedown on his chest.

"What was it like at Gettysburg?"

"Gettysburg." He crooked his elbow over his eyes. He was silent for so long I thought he wasn't going to answer at all. Finally, he said, "I can't begin to describe Gettysburg. I spend my days and nights trying to forget about Gettysburg. But I've heard your mother asking you not to go off to war, Chigger. I've seen you staring at the photographs of your

father and brothers in uniform. I can imagine what you're thinking. What you're trying to decide. I'll try to tell you about Gettysburg. Maybe it will make a difference."

"Don't turn this on me." I didn't like him even guessing some of what was going on inside my heart and head. "Don't—"

"Gettysburg was everything grand and glorious," he began, interrupting me. "And everything...evil, all rolled together..."

The rain began to stream down our windows but soon I was seeing only what Captain George Tallard had seen on the third day of hard fighting at Gettysburg: 12,000 Rebel men lined up to cross an enormous open field toward the waiting Yankees. I saw the flags hanging limp in the muggy heat, felt the enormous pride and grim determination and choking fear that advanced with the Rebels as they began the unprotected march toward what they hoped would be the last fight of the war. And I heard the crashing guns, smelled the smoke and powder, as the Yankees unleashed a hail of lead that in the end left 7,500 Rebels dead or wounded.

"My boys got cut to pieces heading across that field. Every cannon shell that hit the line sent up choking clouds of dust. Flying out of the dust would come arms, guns, heads, knapsacks... And I had to keep going. Just keep going. Even when Louis got killed...I had to keep going forward."

"Who was Louis?" I whispered.

"I got hit by two balls about the same moment," Tallard said, like he hadn't heard my question. "The one that went through my side and the one that shattered my arm bone. It didn't hurt at first. First was the shock. This terrible slam. Suddenly, I was on the ground. I remember being scared that I'd get trampled. I remember crying a bit, thinking of my wife. My children."

I had sunk to the floor beside Tallard's bed. *Soldiers aren't supposed to cry*, I thought, but at the same moment I was wondering if my pa and brothers had thought of us at home while they lay dying on some muddy battlefield, and cried too.

"I thought sure I'd be captured. But Sergeant Krick saw me, and managed to drag me back toward our own lines. He must have gotten me to some field hospital. I was unconscious a good part of the time. A blessing, I guess. Next time I truly came awake my arm was gone and I was getting loaded into an ambulance wagon. I don't know how many ambulance wagons there were—"

"I heard the train was 17 miles long. Some say 10,000 wounded men. Some say 12,000."

"Twelve thousand…" Tallard shook his head. "Well, before the train even began rolling the windows of heaven opened. A fierce hard rain came down. The canvas wagon tops didn't provide any shelter, the wind was blowing so hard. We were all soaked. There was no straw in our wagon—we were just lying on the bare boards—and soon we were lying in pools of water. There was nothing for it. Finally the wagons were in line and we got moving…"

I was gone from that room, with Tallard on that stormy night as the wagon train of wounded jolted over the steep mountain roads. I heard the horses and mules screaming, maddened by the blinding storm, and the shouts of the wagoners trying to manage them. I heard the ferocious flapping of canvas tops torn open by the winds. I heard the wails of agony as the night wore on and the suffering men were banged and bumped over the rocky roads. I heard the cries of the hurting boys:

"My God, have mercy on me! Let me die! Let me die!"

"Someone please, put me out and leave me by the roadside! Please leave me to die in peace!"

Some were praying, some were screaming, some cursing the night, some weeping for loved ones, some begging for water. There were no attendants to help ease the shivering, wounded men's suffering. The exposed wounds were hideous.

After jolting west over the mountains, the wagon train angled south toward the Pennsylvania-Maryland border. Most of the men were glad to see the dawn of July 5th slide wet

Confederate Brigadier General John Imboden was given the dangerous assignment of transporting the wagon train of wounded Confederate soldiers to Williamsport. "The rain fell in blinding sheets," he wrote later. "Canvas was no protection against its fury, and the wounded men...were drenched. Horses and mules were blinded and maddened by the wind and water."

National Archives & Records Administration

over the horizon, but with the light came scattered attacks by Yankee cavalry along the route of the wagon train. The Confederate cavalry, escorting the train, pounded back and forth to meet every threat, but the men lying helpless in the wagons listened to the gunfire and wondered if the next riders they saw would be wearing Yankee blue.

Near Greencastle, Pennsylvania, a mob of Unionist civilians burst from the woods beside the road carrying axes, and began hacking at the spokes on the wagon wheels. "It happened so fast...I heard them yelling at us, and the wagon drivers yelling at them, and then one of the wheels on my wagon collapsed and we all pitched down toward the road in a heap. I landed on my arm, and the pain just swallowed me up and everything went black—"

"Captain Tallard!"

I was miles away from our little log house outside Williamsport, and Tallard was too, and I think we both about jumped out of our skin when a big Rebel burst through our

The Confederate troops retreating from Gettysburg had a hard march in torrential rain.

Sketch by Edwin Forbes

front door. "Captain!" he said again. I finally recognized Sergeant Krick, who had brought Tallard to us a week earlier. The toothbrush was still hanging from his buttonhole. The bruise on his cheek didn't look much improved, still purple and blue and green.

I scuttled away from him, back toward the wall. I noticed that Ma, who had come to the kitchen door at some point during Tallard's tale, disappeared again too.

Krick didn't pay either of us any mind. "Captain, come on," he said urgently, tugging at his friend's good arm. "It's time to go. I've got a wagon outside, and just a couple more stops to make. It's time to get you across the Potomac."

I hugged my arms across my chest. Here it was. Tallard's escape. I'd waited a week for the Yankees to come and scoop him up. It wasn't going to happen. Tallard was going to slip away to freedom after all.

But Captain George Tallard shook his head, confounding Krick and me too. "You'll have to go without me," he said. "I'm staying here."

CHAPTER FOURTEEN

JULY 13, 1863

Sergeant Krick looked like he'd been smacked. "What? Of course you're going. I'll help you—"

"No, I can't." Tallard pulled his arm away. "The surgeon told me I couldn't go. He said another wagon trip, even a short one, would kill me."

Krick's jaw sagged open. "But...but I can't just leave you here! Come on, Captain. You can make it."

"I can't leave."

Krick shook his head as if to clear it. "Sir, I don't have time to argue! You got to come with me now! The Yankees are going to be down on us like fleas on hounds! Do you want to end up in a Yankee prison, or take a chance with your friends?"

Tallard's gaze locked with Krick's. "Go fetch the others. Go."

Krick looked so bewildered I felt sorry for him. "Captain...*George*...I've known you since I was five years old. I followed you to the recruitment tent, and I followed you into Pennsylvania, and I am not planning on leaving you here now! You brought us all this far—don't leave us now—"

97

"I can't go with you. Go get the rest of my boys and get them out of here. That's an order!"

Krick still looked like a lost boy. "George—"

"Go now!" Tallard commanded, his voice hard as iron.

Krick drew a harsh breath, then clasped Tallard's hand. "Good luck. Hang on, my friend. We'll meet again." With a quick nod he turned and clattered back out the door.

Tallard squeezed his eyes shut. For a moment I couldn't move, couldn't even close my dangling jaw. Then a sudden squall of raindrops rattled against the front window. It rattled something inside of me, too.

I jumped to my feet. "What are you doing?" I demanded. "I was here when the surgeon came. I heard what he said. He didn't tell you to stay behind."

Tallard opened his eyes. "Leave this be."

"Leave what be? What are you doing?"

"It's got to stop. Do you understand? It's got to stop."

"No, I don't understand! What's the matter with you?"

"Chigger, listen to me. This war has to stop. The killing has to stop. I thought it might all end here, but it looks like Lee's going to slip away once again, and save his army to fight another day. This war isn't going to end with a big battle, Chigger. Your Yankee generals don't have the stomach for it. It's going to drag on and on. Another year, maybe two, maybe three or four. The way I see it, it won't stop until one side or the other runs out of men. And it's going to be the Confederate side, that's clear. The war isn't going to end until the South doesn't have any more men to stand up and fight."

"But..."

"I don't know how to stop the war. This is all I know to do."

My head felt like the swirl of a Potomac eddy. "How is you staying in Williamsport going to help anything?"

"One less man to fight. One less gun."

"You're done fighting! You can go home to your wife—"

His shook his head. "You think I'm finished just because I lost an arm? I'm an officer. They'll give me a furlough home, but they'll want me back. They can't spare me just because I lost an arm. And I can't do it any more. Don't you understand?"

"If you stay here, the Yankees will come and take you. You'll be hauled off to a Yankee prison."

"I know."

"You won't just sit out the war, you know. You'll die there."

He drew a deep breath. "Maybe not. But…probably so."

I grappled for words. "But what about your family? Your children?"

Tallard picked up his tintype photograph, looked at it with eyes full of pain. "I'm doing this for them," he said. "Lord knows I don't want my wife to suffer widowhood, or my children to grow up without a father. But even more, I don't want them to grow up in the middle of the war. The South is going to be destroyed altogether if this war doesn't stop—"

"That's politician-talk!" I snapped. "*I* grew up in the middle of a war, and I can tell you it would have been a dang sight better if I still had a father. Don't tell me you're thinking of your children, because you surely aren't—"

Tallard grabbed my arm so hard I yelped. "You don't understand. I can't go home. I *can't*. I can't face them all. I recruited that company. They followed *me*. Now most of my boys are dead or dying or in prison. I led those boys onto the field. How can I face their mothers? Their wives?"

I pulled my arm away. "I don't hate the officers my pa and brothers followed. I hate the war. I hate the Rebels who killed them." It flashed through my head what a peculiar argument this was—me arguing with a Reb who *wanted* to get captured—but I couldn't seem to stop. "Go home to your family. Let them tend you while you mend. It'll mean the world."

"I'm a stranger to them now." Tallard covered his eyes with the crook of his elbow again. "The man they knew is already dead. In battle, I've seen things…done things….And now Louis is dead." His voice was raw with pain.

"Who was Louis?" I demanded. And when he didn't answer right away, I shook his arm. "Who was Louis?"

Raindrops hammered the roof. "Louis was my wife's youngest brother," Tallard said finally. "She adored him. And he was like a younger brother to me. After my wife's parents died, Louis came to live with us. When I decided to raise a company, he was crazy to go with me. He was too young— about your age—but he begged and teased so…finally I said yes. My wife didn't want him to go. 'Don't let him, George,' she pleaded. Over and over. But I'd already promised him. 'I'll keep an eye on him,' I told her. I *promised* her. Oh God, why did I let him come?"

For a horrifying moment I thought he was going to bust out bawling. Instead he took a deep, shuddering breath. "I can't go home. Don't you see?"

I rubbed my forehead. "When did you decide to do this?" I was remembering everything I'd wrestled with in the last week…hoping Tallard would bleed to death, hoping a shell would fall on him, hoping he'd be captured and sent to prison camp.

He looked very tired. "I don't know. Maybe it was when I saw that magnificent Southern line—my boys—ripped to pieces on that Gettysburg field. Maybe it was the instant I knew Louis was dead. Maybe it was in the middle of the night on that trip in the wagon train." He waved his hand at the mantel. "Maybe it was hearing about your own dead. Too many dead. Too many widows. Too many orphans." Tallard closed his eyes.

I stared at him, my head pounding. Images flashed through my mind like some crazy magic-lantern picture show. My own pa marching away. Ma in a weeping heap in her muddy mourning dress. My dead brothers, staring down at me from the mantel. Tallard's boy Splinter, staring too, waiting for his pa to come home.

The choices, the decisions, the tug-of-war that had been raging inside for so long were threatening to break me into little pieces. I had to stop thinking. I had to *do*.

"Get up," I ordered Tallard.

"What?"

"Get up!" The confusion was gone, shoved aside by anger. Anger was good. It stilled the voices in my mind and fueled my arms and legs to action. "Did you hear me? Get up!" I grabbed his arm as Krick had, and hauled him to a sitting position.

"What are you doing?" he demanded.

I pulled his legs over the side of the bed. "I'm making sure you get to the river. Now get up!"

"I'm not—"

"*I-said-get-up!*" I hollered. A war's worth of frustration and rage came out in those four words. "You're sick of the dying? Well, I am too! Go home to your family. Go home to your boy."

Tallard jerked away. "I'm not fit to be a father—"

"This isn't all about you! Are you so selfish you'd leave your boy without a pa rather than face up to what you done? Are you such a coward? You don't know what being without a pa does to a boy. *I* know. And I know sure as you're born that you aren't going to just sit here, waiting for the Yankees to haul you off. Not in my house." I yanked Tallard's arm again, and he stumbled to his feet. I don't know if something I said made some sense to him, or if he just figured I'd keep tugging and kicking until he gave way, but he was on his feet.

This was too much for Ma. "Chig don't," she cried from the kitchen door. "Leave him! Leave him for the Yankees!"

"I got to do this, Ma," I grunted. I was trying to figure out how a runt like me could manage a big reluctant wounded man like Tallard.

She stomped one little foot. "Chigger!" Her tone had never failed to stop an O'Malley man before. "That man is our enemy! He killed your brothers and your pa!"

"Don't," Tallard was saying at the same time. "Don't."

"I got to do this," I said again. It was the only answer I could find for either of them. I didn't know if I could get Tallard safely to the Potomac before the Yankees crashed down. But I knew I had to try.

CHAPTER FIFTEEN

JULY 13, 1863

"Chigger, don't do this," Tallard said again as we stumbled down our lane.

"Just hush your trap," I hissed, and he did.

I wasn't planning on doing all that much, actually. I figured if I could just get him down our lane to the main road, I'd find an ambulance or supply wagon to load him into, and that would be the end of it.

But it didn't work out quite so smart. "I can't take on any walking wounded," one driver told me. "Orders."

"But a wagon got sent for him already! He just didn't...didn't make it in that one."

"Orders," the driver said again, like that one word started and ended all discussions. In the army, I guess it did.

The next driver I hollered at said much the same thing. "I already got a full load. If I let him in, I'd have so many stragglers swarming in my poor mules wouldn't be able to take another step."

Half a dozen teamsters refused me, sad or angry or cursing or not caring one way or another. I couldn't understand it.

102

"Chigger," Tallard began again.

"Hold your tongue." I rested his weight against my shoulders, considering. The idea that formed in my head was so hard I forced it away. It bobbed back. "Forget the wagons," I sighed, my heart doing flip flops. "I've got another idea."

We flowed with the traffic for half a mile. I kept Tallard's remaining arm over my shoulders and towed him along. Since he didn't have any coat I had wrapped an old blanket around his shoulders, which got in the way as much as anything else. He stumbled from time to time, and grunted with pain, but his feet kept moving.

None of the other Rebels seemed to notice when we angled off into the woods. Probably thought we were heading off to relieve ourselves, I guess. But Tallard's head came up. "Where are we going?"

"It's not far—watch that branch, now—just through here. I've got a good rowboat hid." *My father's rowboat... Stop thinking. Keep moving.*

"A rowboat?"

"That's what I said. I'm not aiming to row you across. But I'll get you in it, and shove you out good in the current. You'll float down to the bridge at Falling Waters, and someone there will help you. They're hungry for boats. They won't let you go by."

The thought of giving up that rowboat was a stab to the heart. I could fish from the shore...but I could never again recapture the memories of Pa and me out in that boat, together. What would Pa think of me giving it to Tallard? Would his anger reach down from heaven? Or would he see what Tallard had done for Ma, and urge me on?

In the end, my torment was for nothing. Someone had been to the hidden thicket before me. "Crimus!" I swore, staring at the broken branches and trampled underbrush. The boat was gone. "One of your rangy Rebels must have found it." Somehow, having it stolen hurt worse than giving it up. I wanted to rage and cry at the same time.

With a mighty effort, I told myself there was no time to mourn that loss. The daylight was fading.

"Your intentions were kind," Tallard said. "But it didn't work. Just take me back—"

"I'm tired of giving in," I interrupted. This new log of anger just stoked the fire inside. "We'll head in to the Williamsport ford." I began pulling him back toward the road. "It's closest. They're still running the little ferry back and forth. I'll get you on the ferry."

Once on the road, we blended in with the slow tide of men and vehicles pressing toward Williamsport. The gray twilight faded into inky full blackness. The drizzle gave way to another torrential rain—like a river descending from the sky. I'd tugged my old felt hat on before leaving but Tallard had none. I tried to knot the blanket so it stayed hooded over his head, but without a hand to hold it in place, it kept slipping. "Does it ever stop raining here?" he gasped, but kept putting one foot in front of the other.

The closer we got to the ford, the greater the confusion. Nobody seemed to be in charge. Most of the trudging men kept their heads down, stopping or shuffling forward as space required, not asking questions. Some even curled up under rubber blankets and slept. Maybe they were used to the commotion. It tormented me like a biting blackfly. I wanted to finish my business and be done with it.

"I got a wounded man here," I told anyone who would listen…which turned out to be nobody. What was the matter with these people? After a while I quit trying.

Finally we got close enough to spot a couple of men holding hissing torches while other men shouted directions. "Rodes' Division!" one man bellowed. "Rodes' Division, keep going. You'll be wading the river by the mouth of the Conococheague."

I eeled up and grabbed his sleeve. "Sir—"

He shook me off. "Stay with your company. You've got to wade through the aqueduct, then head down the slope to the river."

The aqueduct is a water-filled bridge that allows the C & O Canal and its boats to pass over the Conococheague without getting washed away. I didn't cotton much to the idea of wading it in sunlight, much less in the pouring darkness with a wounded man. "But sir, I got a hurt Reb—"

The officer gave me a shove. "Keep moving!"

"This is wrong," I muttered to Tallard. "We need to cut around these wagons to the main ford. That's where the ferry is." I towed him in the right direction best I could, steering toward the bonfires. It seemed forever before we squeezed across the bridge over the canal and made it to the shore.

For a few moments I stood peering through the downpour at that river. The familiar ford was suddenly strange as a nightmare. Some torch-holding riders were sitting on their horses a few feet out, and more bonfires burned on the Virginia shore. The flames danced spookily on the black water. In the fluttering light I saw men struggling through current that rose to their armpits. They soon disappeared into the darkness. But I could mark the parade by the glint of the dim light sparking on musket barrels and the horses' metal fixings, fading to a glittering thread toward the far shore.

The last wagons were starting out too. Some of the mules were screaming like the devil was on their back, kicking and fighting against heading into that river. I wished Robert was there to help calm 'em down. "They'll rouse the whole Yankee army," I muttered. Then the enormity of what I was doing crashed down again. For an instant I panicked, ready to fling Tallard aside and run home.

What was I doing? What was I hoping for?

Don't think, I ordered myself. Just keep moving. I had to believe I could sort it all out later.

All around me shadowy infantrymen were hanging their cartridge boxes around their necks, and some their shoes too, before wading into the Potomac's black torrent. A few of the Rebs were muttering and cursing the dangerous crossing. But one jaunty group sang "Carry Me Back to Old Virginny" as they stumbled into the water. And someone joked, "Hey, General Lee just knew we was in powerful need of a bath."

One solider—runty, like me—floundered into the water, then splashed right back out. "I ain't tall enough!" he wailed.

"Hurry up, Johnny," one of the other Rebs teased, "or the Yankees will be helping you across."

I shook my head like a wet dog, trying to find some sense in the unnatural night. "I got to get you in the ferry line," I muttered to Tallard. There was no way he could ford the Potomac on foot. Not with his wounds.

I spent another 20 minutes or so fighting through the crowd, getting stepped on and jostled, and keeping a good hang on Tallard. Finally, I heard someone shouting about the ferry, and headed in that direction.

It turned out to be an angry driver. "Look, I got Ewell's artillery here, and orders to get on the ferry." His teams of horses, dragging the heavy guns, blocked the path.

"The ferry is gone!" another man bellowed. His dripping hat was pulled down, so in the darkness he was nothing more than a shadow.

"What do you mean, gone?" the driver demanded. "I got orders—"

"It's gone, I say! I don't know why or how! Maybe the cable broke. Maybe one of the wagons that got swept away snapped it. But it's gone! You'll have to turn around and head for the pontoon bridge at Falling Waters."

"There's no time!" An edge of panic bit at the driver's anger. "The Yankees—"

"I can't help you!" the other man yelled, and melted into the streaming night.

At that particular moment, the full weight of what I'd done pushed down like Troxell's anvil. I'd made a crazy, lightning-fast decision to save Tallard from prison and death. And I'd dragged him out into the storm, fought our way to the ford, only to find there was no way to get him across. And him with one arm, and two bullet holes in his side. Maybe I was killing him after all, more sure than the Yankees.

I didn't know. All I knew was that something, some voice inside, kept driving me on. I'd started down this road. I couldn't give up now.

"Chigger." Tallard sounded tired, and his weight on my thin shoulders was considerable. "Chigger, there's no help for it. Just leave me here."

"Can you still walk?"

"A bit...yes...but—"

"Then come on. We're heading for Falling Waters."

CHAPTER SIXTEEN

JULY 13–14, 1863

I'll never forget the misery of that night march.

The army had passed over the road from Falling Waters on their way to Gettysburg three weeks earlier, and those thousands of tramping feet had kicked up a choking cloud of dust. The past week of almost constant rain had turned that road into what seemed to be a bottomless bog. Frantic horses sank belly-deep in the mud. Artillery rigs and supply wagons mired to their hubs. All these obstacles were no more than shadows in the streaming blackness, but we heard the animals' cries, the pleading riders, the cursing wagoners.

After clawing our way out of Williamsport and heading back downstream, Tallard and I found ourselves in the middle of an endless crush of men. I felt like I had once when I'd fallen from the rowboat while fishing with my father, and the current pulled me along like a helpless twig. Now it was a current of men, Rebel men, engulfing me. I could no more have bucked their flow than sailed to the moon.

Not being able to see any farther than our noses, we all kept a hand on the back of the man in front of us. Sometimes men afraid of getting lost and separated called out the name of their unit: "Fifteenth Georgia!" "Forty-fourth

Alabama!" Sometimes an angry voice in my head—maybe the voices of the dead O'Malleys—demanded to know what I was doing in this river of Rebels. But as the night wore on the voices disappeared. I had all I could do just to keep going.

We'd march for a few steps, then wait a few moments. Take another step or two. Wait. It must have taken an hour to move a hundred paces. Every step was knee-deep in what felt like slushy mud. I stumbled over discarded canteens and stubbed numb toes on broken wagon axles. And all the while the rain beat down like a thousand hammers. Cold water poured down my neck, flowed in my eyes and ears, kept us drenched to the skin.

All crunched together, it was hard to know who was holding up who. Sometimes, when the halts grew too long, we sank waist-deep in the cold ooze to rest. I could tell that men were sleeping as they walked, sleeping as they stood, sleeping when they sat. I didn't know how they managed that until once when someone trod on my foot, and I jerked from some faraway place it took a while to realize had indeed been sleep.

Sometimes I could hear Tallard grunting and gasping beside me. Sometimes he was so quiet I'd feel a jolt of fear, and suddenly wondered if I was towing along a dead man. "You with me?" I'd ask, although the man on the other side of me, or behind or in front of me, was just as likely to answer. Then I'd realize Tallard was still somehow moving his legs, dragging one foot from the sucking mud and planting it in front of the other. His crushing weight was still warm against me.

A gloomy gray daybreak was easing the darkness before we got close to Falling Waters. I was bone-cold and bone-weary and ready to bawl with gladness to see the night end. But no one else was.

"Look back there," someone groaned. "I can see the camp we left last night. It's still in hollering distance."

"Keep it moving," an officer was calling from the side of the road. He was a big man with long beard and tired eyes, mounted on a sagging horse. "Come on boys, move! We got to get you across."

"That's old Pete!" a Rebel near me said. "General Longstreet hisself."

"Ginral, you git yourself across first!" someone else hollered. "Those Yanks are goin' to be cussin' mad when they see most of our army got across during the night. They're comin' for us sure. You git yourself across!"

Some of the men nearby clamored in agreement. That General Longstreet just kept urgently waving us on like errant sheep. "Keep moving, boys! *Keep moving!*"

So we shuffled along. The rain faded off to a misty drizzle. Just as the sun began to peer over the eastern hill, we came in sight of the pontoon bridge.

Now, a normal army pontoon bridge is a marvel to see, neat and tidy. The engineers string together a row of special boats, then build a nice firm wooden road right across the tops, stretching from one riverbank to the other. But this pontoon bridge was a crazy thing of makeshift boats and mismatched timbers, swaying in the current. The wreck of an ambulance wagon, which by the look of things had tumbled right off, was wedged in the water against it. Green willow poles had been laid in the mud leading down to the bridge, I figured in an attempt to keep the wagon and artillery wheels from sinking. But there wasn't anything left but bits of willow and lots of churned mud.

It wasn't much of a bridge, but it was holding. A tight line of wagons was rumbling across in the center, flanked on either side by marching infantry. The men moved slowly on the pitching bridge, struggling to keep their balance. But they were getting across.

I drew a deep, long breath. We'd made it.

Just then Tallard's knees gave, and he sagged to the ground.

That was more than I could countenance. "Come on!" I shouted, trying to get him up. "We're almost there. Don't give up now!"

"I've got to rest," he mumbled. His eyes were closed, his cheeks gray and sunken. Deep new lines of pain seemed carved on his face.

Worry stabbed like a pig-sticker. "Just make it over to those trees," I bargained, and somehow he half-crawled and was half-dragged through the crowd to a little grove of trees nearby. He collapsed on the ground, instantly asleep. Or maybe unconscious, I didn't know. I felt ready to pass out myself, and I didn't have two bullet holes and a missing arm.

I leaned against the peeling bark of a sycamore tree, trying to stay awake. On the road, the gray tide still inched toward the bridge. But we weren't the only stragglers in the grove. There were dozens of men on the ground among the trees, broken-down men too hurt or tired to go any further. Beyond the grove was a little log farmhouse and barn, flying the green flag that meant "hospital." Further back I could see thick earthen embankments built by the Rebels to protect the crossing, topped with some artillery.

I don't know how long we stayed in that grove. I must have dozed myself for a while. Once rested, my mind started turning again on the peculiar questions of how and why I'd come to be in the middle of the Rebel army, helping a wounded Rebel escape, hoping the Yankees would just hold off their attack until he got across. And those questions were so painful I pushed to my feet, trying to leave them behind.

Tallard was still out cold, sucking in quick raspy breaths, as I drifted out for a look-see. Nobody seemed to notice as I wandered behind the farm and climbed up a little hill toward the Rebel fortifications. Some of the infantry posted as rear guards had stacked their guns and were snoring in the mud and puddles. On top of the hill was a clump of men, all peering through field glasses.

"No, no," one of the men was saying. "That's our own cavalry."

"I thought I saw a Union flag, sir."

"Our cavalry boys must have captured another enemy flag," the first man said. "They're shielding our line, Lieutenant. If the Yankees were that close, we'd know about it."

I crept to the top of the hill and squinted out over the field ahead. A squad of cavalry was approaching at a walk. They halted while still a good distance away. It was hard to see much, even the color of their uniforms, in the gray light. But I did see the American flag.

The officer didn't like it. "Those cavalry are dandycock fools," he muttered, loud enough for me to hear. "They capture a flag and have to flaunt it in our faces. Don't they know they're risking having their own men fire on them? Lieutenant, I want you to arrest their leader. I'm going to press charges against him for displaying an American flag at such a time."

But he didn't bring the field glasses down, or move. Neither did the other two men. I suddenly got an odd, crackly feeling down my back—almost like the time a bolt of lightning had struck our stable, and I'd felt the electricity coming a moment or two in advance.

Someone in the distant cavalry column bawled a command, loud enough for us to hear: "Draw sabers!"

A line of steel flashed in the sun. At the same moment I heard the officer nearby let out a long breath. "Oh my God," he said slowly. "They *are* Yankees."

"*Charge!*"

The horsemen pounded straight at us across an open field, yelling, "Surrender, Rebels, surrender!"

"*Yankees!*" someone started bellowing.

And then all hell just busted loose.

I half-ran, half-slid back down the hill toward the grove. Officers behind me were still screaming, "Yankees! Look out! Fire!" Those dozing men of the rear guard jumped up quick, scrambling for their guns and diving for the entrenchments. Shots exploded.

"Gallant charge of the 6th Michigan Cavalry at Falling Waters." One Michigan soldier wrote, "The charge was unsuccessful (as might have been foreseen) and our regiment [was] terribly cut up." A regimental surgeon noted that the charge had "cost us Some of our Bravest & Best men."

Frank Leslie's *Illustrated*, 1863

Some of those Yankee cavalry busted through the line. Pistols were firing. Sabers slicing through the air. One Rebel rider used his gun as a club while he tried to scramble to his saddle. Another Reb grabbed a fence rail and swung it at a Yankee rider in a mighty heave. Some of the Rebels never did reach their guns, and some found their powder was wet, and the guns wouldn't fire. Those men pitched stones at the Yankees, and clawed over the dead and wounded to reach *their* weapons. Men were yelling. Horses were screaming. I heard a *zip zip* sound near my head and realized only a few seconds later it was bullets.

Confederate Brigadier General Johnston Pettigrew was wounded during the charge at Falling Waters, and died three days later in Virginia.

North Carolina Collection,
University of North Carolina
Library at Chapel Hill

I hurtled through the ruckus like a hard-thrown rock. A Yankee howling "Forward Sixth Michigan!" was knocked from his horse, and I swerved around him. I dodged a huge Rebel charging forward like a rabid dog and bellowing "Seventh Tennessee!" like some ancient Irish war cry. When I found myself in the mud my brain screamed, *I'm shot!* but wouldn't allow a stop to my forward motion. I scrabbled on toward the grove. Only later I figured out I'd just tripped.

I was almost to the trees when I saw the flash of a saber off to my right. So I darted left, sudden as a startled rabbit. I didn't see the Rebel rider until I was right in his path. The horse reared, those wicked hooves slicing the air just inches from my head. The Rebel tumbled to the ground heavy as a sack of potatoes.

In that instant I noticed some kind of officer's insignia on his coat. A bandage around one hand. The other hand still tangled in the reins. As the man struggled to free himself a huge Yankee loomed over him. "Surrender!" he demanded, pointing a big pistol at the Rebel officer.

"I will not," the officer gasped. His fingers came free of the reins and reached for his own pistol.

The Yankee fired. Point-blank fired. It caught the officer in the gut, but not before he managed to squeeze off a shot of his own. The Yankee toppled backward like a rag doll. I saw their blood and gore. I smelled the smoke and heard both the din of the fight and the sudden gasps of two dying men. That officer's horse was still pitching like a bee-stung bull.

And I waited for the world to spin, and my stomach to heave, as both had done the day I'd tried to kill Tallard by jerking the pillow from beneath the stump of his arm. But neither happened. Instead, I raced on to the trees.

The peaceful grove was now a storm of confusion. I found Tallard on his feet, staring wildly about. "Come on!" I screamed, grabbing his hand. I pulled. He followed.

Most of the infantry had gotten across the bridge by this time, but those who hadn't were in a panic. The once-patient line now shouted and shoved, across the C & O Canal and on toward the pontoon bridge. I saw a group of scarecrow Rebels, who got pressed against a wrecked wagon blocking the path, lift it up and toss it aside like so much kindling. "Go! Go! Go!" an officer was screaming, and those men didn't pause a lick before stampeding onto the bridge.

I was about to pull Tallard into the fray when my legs stopped so suddenly that a man running behind me gave us a terrible slam. *I can't go on that bridge*, I thought. That notion came as hard and sure as the notion that had commenced me on this unbelievable trip with Tallard in the first place. I knew in my soul that if I crossed that bridge I'd end up in Rebel Virginia, cut off from home. That was more than I could allow.

But Tallard couldn't cross on his own shaky legs, that was certain sure. That tattered bridge was practically whipping back and forth in the current. The last wagoners were screaming at their mules, driving with reckless speed. The charging men on foot were clearly no less set on a single goal: getting their own hides over to Virginia.

Tallard didn't say a word while we stood like a rock in the tide of men. I didn't have breath or energy to explain. I frantically looked left and right, trying to find an answer. Gunfire still crackled behind us. I expected every second to feel a bullet hit, or hear a Yankee soldier bellowing that we were prisoners.

Oh Lord...Ma will skin me alive if I end up in a Yankee prison camp.

The thought was so fearsome and shocking and downright ridiculous that I felt laughter bubbling up inside. Tallard swung his gaze my way, no doubt wondering if I'd gone plum insane. Another ball *zipped* by my left ear.

"Make way!"

Tallard and I stumbled aside as a wagon jolted past. The driver was whipping his mules and men were hanging from the backboard. I had thought all the wounded were already across, but I caught a glimpse of bloody bandages and heard groans of pain as the wagon passed. And when it lurched down the rutted approach ramp, one of the wounded tumbled right off.

The top half of the man's face was wrapped in a dirty bandage. The blind man scrambled to his feet right away, then stood with spread legs and waving hands. "Help me?" he called, then louder, "Help me! Someone help me!"

I dragged Tallard down the slope. "Here!" I yelled, and grabbed the blind Rebel's arm. He was a tall man, and had as much meat on his bones as any of the hungry Rebs. Quickly I wrapped his arm around Tallard's waist. "This man lost his left arm, and is about done-in," I gasped. "But he can see right as rain." I looked quickly from one to the other. "You two got to get each other across the bridge. Understand?"

"Yessir," the blind man said right away. Tallard opened his mouth, his eyes locked on mine. No words came.

"Go!" I screamed. They stumbled down the hill. I kept them in sight as they struggled onto the pitching bridge and started across. Then they got swallowed in the crowd.

CHAPTER SEVENTEEN

JULY 14–15, 1863

That Yankee cavalry charge caught the Rebels by surprise. But they recovered quick, and soon discovered that it was a mighty small group of Yankee riders, all things considered, that had plunged down through the Rebel line. Some said it was a daredevil charge. Some said it was a suicide charge.

It was over in five minutes, although it seemed like death's eternity at the time. But by the time I'd seen Tallard and the other Reb safely on the bridge, that first Yankee charge was done. I heard later that about one hundred Yankee cavalrymen had broken through. Only 30 escaped, bolting back toward their own army. One whole squad of Michigan riders was killed or wounded or captured. The Confederates lost only one Tennessee private and the officer I saw killed. General Pettigrew, his name was.

That rear line of Rebels, the ones who'd fought off those Michigan troopers, had bought the Confederate army the precious minutes they needed. Once the Yankees had withdrawn, the men of the Rebel rear guard scampered down to the bridge themselves. As the last Rebels crossed that crazy pontoon bridge, it was whipping back and forth

118

in the current like an angry snake. I crouched on the Maryland shore, watching, and I heard more yells behind me. Another column of Yankee cavalry, bigger this time, pounded down the hill toward the river, waving their sabers.

Someone on the Virginia side—I heard later it was General Lee himself—ordered that the bridge be cut loose. In the blink of an eye that bridge was loose in the current, breaking apart, sailing downstream. A few boats stayed hooked together on the Maryland side, but they banged up against the shore, no good to anyone.

Those Yankee riders were fighting mad. They bellowed and cursed. Some shook their fists. A few fired some shots across the river, and the Rebels lobbed a few our way. But it was all half-hearted. The real struggle was over.

One of the Yankees dismounted and threw his hat on the ground, kicked at the mud, then glared at me. "Boy, did they all escape?" he asked harshly. I guess he just didn't want to believe what his eyes were telling him.

"Yes," I said slowly, and to tell the truth, I was still taking it all in myself. Then I looked him in the eye and asked a question of my own. "And what in blazes took you so long?"

He didn't answer.

It took me a while to get home. I was threshing time-tired, for one thing. For another, the Falling Waters Road was still clogged with soldiers. Yankee soldiers, this time. They milled about, rounding up some Rebel prisoners who'd straggled or been sleeping or gotten cut off somehow. They didn't bother me, a mud-caked runty boy in farm clothes with no gun. And you know, I hardly took notice of them. My body was tired but my head was full of more thoughts than fleas on a stray hound.

When I finally limped down our lane, I noticed two spare-ribbed mules standing in our yard, heads hung low, looking too beat to move. Then I noticed another broken-down mule by the house. I'd seen a few other such pathetic creatures on my walk home. They were harness animals too starved and tired to pull another army wagon, and left behind by the retreating Confederates. But I couldn't figure how three had ended up in our yard.

Robert appeared around the corner. He patted the closest mule, then noticed me and bounded over. "Chig! Say, you look awful."

"Hello, Robert. You want to sleep in the stable tonight?" I was too tired to make much more of him being there.

"Well, I did come to use your stable, Chigger. That is, if I can. I can, can't I? Please?"

Something in his tone cut through my haze. Robert was excited, or anxious, about something. "What for?"

"The mules! They left 'em, Chigger. Can you believe it? I asked one of the Rebels last night if the army wanted 'em, and he said, 'I wouldn't waste a bullet on one of those mules.' Can you believe it? I've got these here, and two more already in the stable."

It seemed a bad idea and I hesitated, remembering how he'd grieved for his stolen canalboat mules. I didn't want to see his heart break again. "Robert...I think the reason they got left behind is that they're so broken-down. They're of no use to anybody. They'd probably drop over sideways-dead if you blew on 'em—"

"But I can tend 'em, Chig!" he interrupted anxiously. "I know I can. All's I need is a place to house 'em, since my old place got washed away. I need your stable."

I chewed my lip. "The roof's falling in," I finally reminded him.

"I know. All's they need is one good corner, and we got that."

"I don't have any hay. What're you going to feed them?"

"They can browse for now. And I'll cut hay for the winter. I can do it."

I knew he could. Besides...it suddenly occurred to me that Robert might just be offering me a way out of one of my own problems. I slapped him on the arm. "Sure, Robert. You can use the stable. We don't have any stock left anyway. If anybody can bring those tired old mules back around, it's you."

Robert grinned like the sunrise.

I heard him sweet-talking one of those old mules as I turned back to the house. Ma was standing in the door, waiting. I guess she'd heard me talking to Robert. I sucked in a deep breath and went to meet her.

I couldn't tell if she was angry or disappointed or what. "So," she said finally. "Did the Reb get across the river?"

"I guess so. I think so."

Ma and I had a lot of talking to do. But I was too beat to do it just then, and I guess she saw so in my eyes. "I got hot water on the stove," she said, stepping aside so I could come in the house. "Go wash up. I'll find you a dry shirt."

Mud was crusted between my toes. Up my shirt. In my hair. Before even starting in on the hot water, I had a pile of mud chips on the floor.

"I'm feeling like I ought to take a hog scraper to you," Ma said from the kitchen door. For one scared moment I thought she was serious. Then my tired brain realized she was making a joke. And I knew that although Ma may not have understood why I'd helped Tallard, I was forgiven.

I slept all that day and well into the night, back on my regular pallet in the corner. When I woke, sometime in the black of night, I heard Ma's breathing from her own bed. I figured she must have boiled the devil out of her bedsheets, after me and Tallard left. Boiled Tallard right out of them.

Tallard.

Suddenly I was wide awake. Where was he? Had he and his blind companion safely made it across the bridge? Was he resting in some Virginia field hospital, safe on his own soil? Or had our trek through the storm sapped the last bit of strength he had? Was he alive or was he dead?

And I saw again, over and over, that Confederate General Pettigrew getting gut-shot right in front of me. He hadn't died quick, but he was surely dead by now. Would his horse have reared if I hadn't run in its path? Would that general be alive right now, leading his men on some Virginia road? Would his widow be saying prayers of thanks, instead of screaming out her grief?

Tallard had tried to get captured so the war would have one less soldier, one less gun. I had tried to give Tallard back to his army. Had I given the Confederate army a common foot soldier and killed off a general?

What had I done?

Was it God's way of saying the Yankees were right, and He didn't want me to give Tallard back?

Was it vengeance from the dead O'Malleys, looking down from heaven angry because I had helped one of the enemy?

For one long moment, there in the blackness, I thought my very head would burst like a cannon shell from trying to figure out the war. Somewhere in the distance outside a dog barked. I pressed my fists against my forehead.

No.

I don't know where the answer came from, but just as sudden, I had it. Surely God hadn't reached down, or an O'Malley either, and pushed me in the path of that general's horse. Now that I'd had a tiny taste of being in the middle of the war—not just cowering in the root cellar—I understood such things better.

The war was a huge, ugly thing beyond the understanding of any single man, tearing out of control like a runaway horse. No one man could make a choice that would bring it to a halt. In the end, all a body could do was rely on his sense of right and wrong. Tallard had done us a kindness. I'd repaid in turn.

Suddenly, something Father Ryan had said during his last visit echoed through my mind: *Sometimes the simplest act of kindness can mean the most.* I remembered how much I had appreciated him taking a few minutes to walk down to our place and talk to Ma, and to me. I remembered how I'd felt when Robert shared his bag of food with us. Not just grateful, but...less angry. Less filled with hate.

Maybe, in the end, people doing little kindnesses as the chance arose might help bring the war to an end.

I guess it sounds simple. But during wartime, a man needs a...a plan to guide his hand. He can't just spin like a weathervane in the wind. I'd been spinning ever since Liam left home. It was time to find my direction.

Since Tallard was gone, Robert sat down to breakfast with me and Ma the next morning. After he'd headed back out, Ma faced me across the table.

"Chigger," she said, "about that Rebel. Why'd you do it? Why?"

I'd been waiting for the question. "Maybe it was that infernal photograph of his," I began slowly. "I don't know that you ever looked close upon it...but his children, his family, they had the saddest old hound dog eyes you ever saw."

"Sadder than this house? He and his kind—"

"I *know* what they did," I interrupted her. I wouldn't tolerate her suggesting I had forgotten my dead father and brothers.

I could tell she wasn't moved, so I plunged on ahead. "Mostly, though, it was on account of him helping us. Sending off those Rebels who were going to rough you up, that day you threw all the kitchen fixings at them—"

"I'd do it again."

"And he told me to just up and fetch Willis and bring him to you. That was his idea, Ma."

"Well, I'm not knowing that it was any of his concern," she huffed.

"I was losing you, Ma. I couldn't see...anything left inside you but—but hatred and fear, and not much of that. Mostly I wasn't seeing anything. It scared me. The first spark of...of *life* I saw in way too long came when I put Willis in your arms. That was Tallard's idea, Ma. Tallard's."

She didn't find any more to say.

I leaned toward her. "You know what, Ma? I don't know why I helped Tallard. But I do know that it was the right thing to do. I just know." And that's the first thing I've known for sure in a long time, I wanted to add, but I could tell she was still struggling to accept my choice. I needed to give her some time before finishing this conversation.

"I'm going to town to get the news," I told her, and left her to her thoughts.

The road was busy with Yankees in Union blue. I kept to the edge of the road, staying out of their way, but couldn't help feeling better just to see them. They were noisy and dirty, and slow as cold molasses lately. But they were still *my* army, the O'Malley's army, and I was glad they were here.

Robert had been up on Cemetery Hill the morning before, while I was at Falling Waters, and had seen them advance. "You never saw such a sight," he'd told us at breakfast that morning, his voice hushed with awe. The huge line had marched toward Williamsport in formal battle array, row upon row of tidy ranks marching in step. Flags fluttered in the breeze. Guns glistened in the sunlight. Some soldiers were detailed to clear the way in front of the line, ripping down fences and stone walls and outhouses so the thousands of soldiers could march in perfect formation through yellow wheat fields and meadows of green clover. The whole Army of the Potomac had advanced for two miles in that line of battle, column by column, ten lines deep. It was a glorious sight.

The Yankees had advanced on Williamsport ready, finally ready, for the big battle that would end the war. Instead they found, of course, empty fortifications, and the Rebels gone. I shook my head, thinking it all over as I turned onto East Potomac Street. Maybe one day I'd understand what had taken the Yankees so long. I didn't yet.

As I turned the corner, my feet slowed. What was I doing here? I had nowhere to go. I'd come walking out of habit. But, I realized, I didn't need to walk any more. Walking, endless walking for miles and days and years on end, was for boys trying to escape from something. I wasn't bent on escaping any more.

"Chigger!" Father Ryan stood on the church steps, broom in hand, and I swerved around a bunch of Yankees lounging near the steps to join him. "It's good to see you, lad! I've been wondering how you and your mother were faring."

"Well enough, Father. And you?"

He shook his head sadly, gesturing to the church. "We've quite a mess, I'm afraid. Half the pews ripped out, blood stains on the floor... But we'll clean it up. We'll rebuild."

"I'll give you a hand," I offered, and was rewarded by the smile that lit his face.

The sanctuary was a mess, sure enough. It felt good to have something to lay into without doubt or regrets. And I was glad enough to have a chance to talk to the priest. "Father Ryan, I want to tell you something my ma doesn't even know yet."

"Yes?"

We were hauling out planks that had been nailed over pews to make raised beds for some of the wounded. "I'm heading out. When the Yankees leave, I'll be leaving with them."

"Chigger!" The priest stopped and let his end of the plank bang to the floor. "You're too young—"

"I'm not enlisting as a soldier. But they've got plenty need for willing workers. I can drive mules. Help cook, or wash dishes. Help the surgeons. Whatever they need." I put my end of the plank down too, since he wasn't moving.

"Oh, Chigger." Father Ryan bowed his head for a moment. "Why are you doing this?"

"Because I have to," I answered. There among the wreckage of the sanctuary, I told him what I'd done to help Tallard get across the river, and why. "I guess I'll never know for sure if it was the right thing to do," I finished slowly. "But I think it was."

"I think it was too," Father Ryan said softly. "Don't be letting anyone say otherwise."

"So now…heading out with the Yankee army feels like the right thing to do, too. Maybe part of it is to let my father and brothers know that even though I helped the Rebel Tallard, I believe in what they did. What they died for. I'm proud of their memory."

"I'm sure they know that, Chig."

"But mostly, I just want to help. Maybe even find ways to do some kind turns, this time for my own soldiers. I can't make any sense of the war, Father. All I know to do is try to help out. Maybe make things easier for some other boy's father, or brother."

Father Ryan's eyes were dark with worry. "It's a good thing you're thinking of, such as it goes. But what of your poor mother?"

"I need to find work one way or another, and there's no jobs for me in Williamsport. I was about torn in half, trying to figure how to do that and still keep Ma going. But everything's worked out. She'll be staying with Agnes, at the big house on Clear Spring Road. She'll have baby Willis to help mind, every day, which will help a lot." I paused, and a burst of laughter from the soldiers outside drifted through the open windows. I could tell Father Ryan was thinking everything over.

"I'm telling you this because I need you to look in on her," I told him. "Agnes and her folks are Methodist. Ma will need you."

"Of course I'll look in on her," he said. But the worry in his eyes didn't fade.

"She's doing better," I added, as we picked up the plank and started back outside. "She'll be well."

And as I edged down the steps of the battered little church, I prayed I was right. It was the only thing I wasn't sure of.

CHAPTER EIGHTEEN

JULY 15–19, 1863

I can't say Ma took the news well.

"No!" she cried. She grabbed both of my shoulders and gave me a good shake. Just as quick she let go and took a step backwards, hands clutched over her heart. "Chigger, you're just a boy. My boy. The only boy I have left! How can you do this to me!"

"I'm not doing this to hurt you. I'm doing this because it's what I need to do."

"You're leaving me all alone!"

"You won't be all alone, Ma. You can go stay with Agnes. She wants you to come, truly. And Robert is going to stay here with his mules. He can keep an eye on the place while you're in town."

Ma's face crumpled. "Chigger...I need you here, I need you to keep going."

"We can't keep going like this anyway, Ma. That's the truth. The garden's empty. The stable's empty. I don't know how to provide for you. I'd have to leave home anyway, and try to find work. Agnes's offer was generous, but if I went with you, I wouldn't have anything to do there. I can't just...just wander. Besides, me leaving gives them one less mouth to feed."

"You're all I have!"

"No I'm not," I said, real firm. "You have Willis. He needs a grandmother like you. He needs a grandmother who can tell him tales of Ireland, and make sure he knows all about Liam, and play him lullabies on the fiddle when he has nightmares."

"Willis can't take Liam's place. Willis can't take your place."

"No. But he needs you, just the same."

The tears came then, spilling over and streaking down her cheeks. "Chigger, please. I need *you*, need you to keep going—"

"No you don't!" Lordy be, it was hard to speak to her in such a manner, but I had to. "Ma, I can't keep you going. You've suffered terribly, sure enough. Your heart's been broken over and over. But Ma...you got to find something inside yourself to keep getting you out of bed in the morning. It's got to come from you."

She pressed her hands against her eyes, sinking down on the kitchen bench.

I grabbed her shoulder this time, trying to make her listen. To *hear.* "Ma, ever since Pa and Egan died, and especially since Patrick and Liam died too, you and I haven't been really living. We've been hiding from the war. We've been...we've been retreating, sure as those consarned Rebels worked so hard to retreat from Gettysburg. I haven't known what to do, so I haven't done anything. I felt like you wanted me to stay home, and Pa and the boys would want me to enlist for them and for Ireland and for the cause or whatever. And I couldn't choose, so I didn't do anything."

"You've chosen now." Her voice was bitter. But at least she was still talking.

"It's not like I've chosen Pa's side over yours. I can't make a choice because I think it's what Pa would do. I've chosen what seems right for me."

"But why?" she wept. "What good will it do? You're just a boy!"

Tallard's voice echoed suddenly in my mind: *One less gun. One less man.* "I believe one man can make a difference," I told her. "Even one runty boy, trying to do the right thing. Trying to help. Looking for ways to do a kindness here and there."

Her shoulders shook with sobs.

I hesitated, then, "I'd like your blessing, Ma."

"I won't be giving it!" She wouldn't look at me.

I took a deep breath. Well, fair enough. Still, our talking wasn't done. I sank on the bench beside her, desperate to break through. "Ma, I won't be carrying a gun. I'll do everything I can to stay safe, and get home to you in one piece when this cursed war is done. But Ma…I need to know you're going to be well. Do you understand? I need to know you're going to…to not disappear inside yourself. Can you just promise me that?"

But it was too much to ask. I patted her shoulder, and sat beside her, and finally left her to cry herself out.

The bulk of the Yankee army didn't cross the Potomac in tardy pursuit of the Rebels for several days. Before they got all set to go, I went out to the camps to see about finding me a place. "You're too young," one man with bushy sidewhiskers blustered. "Too small," another officer laughed, waving his hand like I was a lost puppy.

But I kept wandering, and soon found a home. "You want to come with us, boyo?" a stocky man asked, squinting over a smelly cigar. His Irish lilt was a comfort. So was the green flag at the end of the row of tents. My father and brothers had followed that flag.

I nodded hard. "I'm small," I allowed. "But I'm sturdy."

"Are y'sure you're up to it? War's no easy thing, laddie."

A week ago, I wouldn't have known. But now—after my night march with Tallard, after seeing General Pettigrew gutshot right in front of me, and after managing to keep moving, keep thinking, after both of those things—yes. "I'm up to it. And I want to help."

"Your pa know you're here?"

I laid out the facts. "My pa and my brother Egan died at first Bull Run. My brother Patrick died at Antietam Creek. And my brother Liam died at Chancellorsville. In the Irish Brigade, all of 'em."

"Oh, lad…" The man threw the cigar on the ground and clapped an arm around my shoulders. "Sure, then, you march on with us. We've got plenty of camp chores for a boy like you."

And so it was done.

I climbed Cemetery Hill to visit the silent O'Malleys, and I stopped to say good-bye to Agnes and Willis, and to Father Ryan. There was no one else, really. Robert had already promised to mind the home place while Ma and I were both gone.

On the morning I needed to leave, I told my mother I'd walk her to Agnes's. "No," she said, in a tone that brooked no argument. "I'll see you off from my own home." I had wanted to know she was safe with Agnes—not all alone—before leaving, but she wouldn't give in.

I stuffed a spare shirt and jacket in a sack, and laced on my shoes. That was all there was to it. "Good-bye, Ma," I said, with a fierce hug. "Try not to worry."

Her hug almost choked the breath right out of me.

"Are you going to manage?" The words burst from me. I knew I was doing the right thing…but I was also desperately hungry for just this one reassurance. "Are you going to be well?"

She opened her mouth, then closed it again as if she didn't trust herself to speak. Unshed tears wet her eyes. "Go," she finally managed, then clamped her mouth shut like she never planned to open it again.

It was even harder than I'd expected to turn my back and walk away. My newfound certainty fled like the Rebels. Was I being foolish? Was I being cruel—

The sound cut across the sulky morning air. I stopped, rooted like an oak tree. The tone was almost forgotten, yet hauntingly familiar. It was hesitant and sad and somehow still full of life.

My mother was playing her fiddle.

I stood rock-still and let the music fill the yard. Fill *me.* Tears blurred my sight but it didn't matter. All I needed to do was listen.

After a moment I placed the tune. It was a new recruiting song for the Irish Brigade, "My Father's Gun":

> Come listen now, I'll tell you how I came to leave
>   Killarney, O,
> I'm one of the boys that fears no noise, and me name is
>   Paddy Kearney, O,
> My father's name it was the same, and my grandfather
>   before him, O,
> He carried this gun in '98, when the green flag floated
>   o'er him, O!
>
> When the Rebels raised a hullabaloo, and of Sumpter
>   took possession, O,
> Instead of our flag, they raised a rag—the standard of
>   secession, O,
> It's then I joined the 69th, my father's gun to shoulder, O,
> For meself, you know, can slaughter the foe—no devil
>   of one is bolder, O!
>
> Then O, what fun, to see them run, and to leave a name
>   in story, O!
> With my father's gun I'll follow the drum, and fight my
>   way to glory, O!

I tucked every note into my memory, to hear again later. It didn't matter that I wasn't carrying my father's gun, or that I wasn't going to "slaughter the foe." Ma had found a way to tell me she understood a bit of why I was leaving.

And she'd found a way, the very best way, to tell me she'd still be on her feet when I got back to her.

I waited until the last note faded away. Without turning around, I raised a hand in salute. Then, I marched on down the lane.

Yankee troops crossing the C & O Canal and Potomac River in pursuit of the Confederates. Note the soldier at front left, detailed to keep civilian onlookers at a safe distance.

Painting by David Blythe; courtesy National Baseball Hall of Fame Library, Cooperstown, New York.

AFTERWARD

The war dragged on for two more years. I saw more hurt and hardship than I can ever tell. The Irish Brigade fought on, at terrible places like the Wilderness and Cold Harbor and Petersburg. But I kept my head down, and helped out best I could. I wrote letters for hurt men, and chopped firewood, and cleaned up hospital messes for the surgeons. I like to think I made a difference. When times got really bad, I'd close my eyes at night and call up the memory of Ma's last fiddle tune. It helped keep me going.

And when it was all over, I went home to Williamsport. Willis hid behind a chair until his mother and grandparents coaxed him to come out and meet his uncle. My mother wept and hugged me and wept again. Then, she played her fiddle well into the night. We all sang and sniffled and sometimes danced a bit, and sang some more.

I never saw Tallard again. But after I got home, Robert gave me a tiny parcel that had been shoved under our door some time in 1864. When I pulled away the brown paper I found a tintype.

George Tallard was sitting in a chair, his empty sleeve pinned up neat. His wife was behind him, one hand resting on his shoulder. A tall boy—Splinter—stood with a hand on

Tallard's other shoulder. And a girl—Eliza, wasn't it?—was pressed against his knee. They all looked half-starved. This was late wartime in the South, after all. But I looked at Tallard's eyes and imagined he was trying to tell me something. *Thank you*, his eyes said. I made it, and my family's going to make it too.

Sometimes I look at the photograph and still feel angry, knowing this Rebel family survived the war together when so many of my own loved ones are dead. But I keep it to remind myself that once, in a tight spot, I'd scraped up the courage and conviction to act like a decent man. And mostly, it makes me smile.

AUTHOR'S NOTE

When most people think of the Gettysburg campaign, they think of the battle ending on the Pennsylvania fields. Even many books devoted to the campaign refer only briefly—if at all—to the fighting that took place in western Maryland as the Confederates tried frantically to hold off Union forays until they could cross the Potomac. The flooding was unprecedented, even to longtime area residents. "The highest water ever known," Otho Nesbitt reported from nearby Clear Spring, where local creeks overflowed their banks. Nesbitt described in his diary how women had been carried clear of the floodwaters in wagons and on horseback.[1]

Under the circumstances, it for a time seemed inevitable—at least to many of the Union soldiers—that the Confederate army would meet their final disaster. One Yankee soldier wrote in a letter, "We have destroyed [the Confederates'] pontoon bridges over the Potomac...The Rebel Army is in a bad state, and there is no telling how they are going to get out of it. It looks as if [General] Lee might be used up."[2] Once sure of victory, the Yankees were shocked when they realized the Confederate army had escaped after all. "I cannot describe my feelings of disappointment and

135

discouragement," wrote one. "A week before it was expected that the fight would be renewed and the escape of [General] Lee's army impossible."[3]

I relied on soldiers' accounts to paint a picture of Williamsport during those difficult days. A chaplain serving with the 7th Virginia Infantry wrote, "The houses are all riddled and almost all deserted, and the country for a mile about is fetid with beef offal and dead horses."[4] John Casler of the 33rd Virginia Infantry helped repair the boats needed to help the Rebels escape. "When we got the boats made we got some tar and borrowed the wash kettles around town to boil it in," he wrote. "The old women wanted to raise a row when we took their kettles, but we promised to bring them back; but we didn't."[5]

Brigadier General John D. Imboden, who was given the difficult task of bringing the wagon train of wounded Confederate soldiers safely from Gettysburg to Williamsport, described the nightmarish trip the wounded men endured. He also wrote, "I required all the families [in Williamsport] to go to cooking for the sick and wounded on pain of having their kitchens occupied by my men for that purpose"; and described the wagoners' fight, ferrying the wounded to safety across the Potomac, and other details of his days in Williamsport.[6]

The prominent military officers mentioned in this story—Confederate Generals Lee, Longstreet, Pickett, and Imboden—were involved in the campaign as indicated. General Johnston Pettigrew was shot as described during the cavalry charge at Falling Waters. He survived long enough to cross the bridge, but died three days later. Captain Tallard, Sergeant Krick, and Surgeon Hatfield are fictional.

Chigger O'Malley and his family are also fictitious. I created them to reflect the lives of hundreds of laboring-class Irish immigrants who made their way to western Maryland to work along the C & O Canal. Famine in Ireland pushed more than a million desperate immigrants to America between 1846 and 1854. Most settled in impoverished urban areas. Others dug canals, built railroads, or excavated mines.

When the Civil War began, poverty was enough to prompt some Irish-Americans to enlist. Some believed they should fight to uphold the country which had provided them a new home. Others enlisted with hopes of proving their worth to those Protestant Americans who had not welcomed the flood of poor Irish-Catholic immigrants. Still others dreamed of gaining military experience that would later help them return to Ireland and fight for freedom from British oppression.

Although thousands of Irish-Americans fought in other Union regiments (as well as the Confederate army), the Irish Brigade was distinctive because it allowed the men to preserve their Irish-Catholic identity. The 69th New York State Militia was one of the many 90-day companies formed when everyone expected the war to end quickly, and fought at the Battle of Bull Run (also called the Battle of Manassas) on July 21, 1861. After that battle, when the army was reorganized, Thomas Meagher decided to form an entire brigade of 2,500 men, all of Irish descent. The new 69th New York State Volunteers became the core unit of the Irish Brigade, which also included the 63rd and 88th New York Regiments, and later other units as well. The Irish Brigade fought with distinction at many of the Civil War's bloodiest battles: Fair Oaks, Malvern Hill, Antietam, Fredericksburg, Chancellorsville, Gettysburg, the Wilderness, Spotsylvania Court House, Cold Harbor, Petersburg. After the Battle of Chancellorsville, in May 1863, less than 500 able-bodied soldiers remained, and recruiting began again. Of the approximately seven thousand men who fought in the Irish Brigade during the war, only about a thousand escaped wounding or death.

Williamsport is a canal town. Nestled at the confluence of the Conococheague Creek and Potomac, aided by the good ford to Virginia, it was a lively village even before the C & O Canal was built in the 1830s. But the canal brought commerce and some prosperity to business owners, and work to the laboring class.

The Civil War changed all that. Williamsport's location provided ready access to troops from both armies. Mills and warehouses were burned by Yankee soldiers to keep goods from Confederate hands. The Confederates made frequent raids upon the canal itself, hoping to disrupt Yankee traffic. Many citizens moved away. Divided loyalties among those who remained created bitter tensions. According to the 1860 census, the town of Williamsport was home to 881 white residents, 119 free blacks, and 22 slaves. Figures aren't available for 1863, but the town's population had probably changed dramatically.

I tried to note business names accurately for the period, but have made some concessions for clarity. For example, the Williamsport Catholic church was consecrated in 1851, but the congregation wasn't known as St. Augustine's until a second building was built in 1876. And although the state of West Virginia had just been created, it became clear from period accounts that civilians and soldiers alike still called the southern shore of the Potomac "Virginia," so I did as well.

If you visit Williamsport today, you can walk the streets of a small town which has not been significantly altered since the Civil War. Stroll the old streets and try to pick out buildings that stood during the Civil War. Cemetery Hill is worth exploring; several cannon still mark the spot where Union artillerymen once occupied the heights. The grassy flat near the ford, where the Confederate soldiers struggled so desperately to return to Virginia, is now a peaceful picnic area (enjoy lunch or a soccer game, but don't wade in the Potomac; the currents are unpredictable and dangerous). Stop by the National Park Service Visitor Center, housed in an old warehouse by the basin that once served busy canalboat traffic. Take a hike along the C & O Canal towpath, which crosses the Conococheague on the now-dry aqueduct. You'll find a terrain much like that Chigger walked in this story.

Notes to Pages 135–136

1. Otho Nesbitt, Diary, July 8, 1863, Clear Spring District Historical Association, Clear Spring, Maryland.
2. John Baille McIntosh, Letter, Brown University Library; USMHI Collections; Gettysburg National Military Park Vertical Files.
3. Luther S. Towbridge, Letter, Gettysburg National Military Park Vertical Files.
4. Annette Tapert, ed., *The Brothers War: Civil War Letters to their Loves Ones from the Blue and Gray* (New York: Times Books, Random House, 1988), p. 152. Letter from Florence McCarthy, serving as chaplain for the 7th Virginia Volunteer Infantry.
5. John O. Casler, *Four Years in the Stonewall Brigade* (Girard, Kansas: Appeal Publishing Company, 1906), p. 179.
6. John D. Imboden, "The Confederate Retreat from Gettysburg," *Battles and Leaders of the Civil War*, vol. iii (New York: Century Publishing Company), pp. 425–27.

ADDITIONAL RESOURCES

BOOKS

Beller, Susan Provost. *Never Were Men So Brave: The Irish Brigade During the Civil War.* New York: Margaret K. McElderry Books, 1998. Suitable for younger readers, this text provides enough background about Irish history to put the formation of the Irish Brigade, and its accomplishments, into context.

High, Mike. *The C & O Canal Companion.* Baltimore: Johns Hopkins University Press, 1997. This well-illustrated guidebook combines local history and a mile-by-mile guide to the C & O Canal National Historical Park.

Kohl, Lawrence, and Margaret Cosse Richard. *Irish Green and Union Blue: The Civil War Letters of Peter Welsh.* Bronx, N.Y.: Fordham University Press, 1986; and O'Brien, Kevin E., ed. *My Life in the Irish Brigade: The Civil War Memoirs of Private William McCarter, 116th Pennsylvania Infantry.* Mason City, Iowa: Savas Publishing, 1996. Both of these provide insight into the experience of the common soldiers in the Irish Brigade. Appropriate for middle school readers or above.

Schildt, John. *Roads From Gettysburg.* Shippensburg, Pa.: Burd Street Press, 1998. Schildt focuses on the final days of the Gettysburg campaign, a period overlooked by many writers.

MUSIC

Kincaid, David. *The Irish Volunteer. Songs of the Irish Union Soldier, 1861– 1865.* Salem, Maine: Rykodisc, 1998. Kincaid's CD brings the music of Union Irish soldiers back to life, including all the songs referenced in this story; lyrics and background information are also provided.

TO PLAN A VISIT

For general information about the C & O Canal National Historic Park, contact: C & O Canal NHP Headquarters, Box 4, Sharpsburg, Md., 21782; phone (301) 739–4200. To reach the C & O Canal Visitor Center in Williamsport, contact: 205 W. Potomac St., Williamsport, Md., 21795; phone (301) 582–0813.

For information about the Gettysburg National Military Park, contact: Gettysburg NMP, 97 Taneytown Rd., Gettysburg, Pa., 17325; phone (717) 334–1124.

— THE AUTHOR —

Kathleen Ernst is the acclaimed author of two previous books for children. Reviewers have praised *The Night Riders of Harpers Ferry* and *The Bravest Girl in Sharpsburg*, both continuing best sellers.

— ALSO BY KATHLEEN ERNST —

THE NIGHT RIDERS OF HARPERS FERRY

Ideal for preteens who desire to experience the excitement of the Civil War, this is a memorable tale of loyalty and adventure, based on a true story.

THE BRAVEST GIRL IN SHARPSBURG

Learn how the Civil War divided friends and tested courage from the experiences of real teenage girls whose hometown lay at the center of conflict in September 1862.

CHECK YOUR LOCAL BOOKSTORES
FOR THESE OTHER WHITE MANE KIDS TITLES

THE SECRET OF THE LION'S HEAD
Beverly B. Hall
ISBN 0-942597-92-3 • SC $7.95

THE NIGHT RIDERS OF HARPERS FERRY
Kathleen Ernst
ISBN 1-57249-013-6 • SC $7.95

BROKEN DRUM
Edith Morris Hemingway and Jacqueline Cosgrove Shields
ISBN 1-57249-027-6 • SC $8.95

BROTHERS AT WAR
Margaret Whitman Blair
ISBN 1-57249-049-7 • SC $7.95

THE BRAVEST GIRL IN SHARPSBURG
Kathleen Ernst
ISBN 1-57249-083-7 • SC $8.95

SHENANDOAH AUTUMN
Mauriel Phillips Joslyn
ISBN 1-57249-137-X • SC $8.95

HOUSE OF SPIES
Margaret Whitman Blair
ISBN 1-57249-161-2 • SC $8.95

REBEL HART
Edith Morris Hemingway and Jacqueline Cosgrove Shields
ISBN 1-57249-186-8 • SC $8.95

WHITE MANE PUBLISHING CO., INC.

To Request a Catalog Please Write to:
WHITE MANE PUBLISHING COMPANY, INC.
P.O. Box 152 • Shippensburg, PA 17257